TOMB OF RELICS

AN ARKANE THRILLER
J.F. PENN

Tomb of Relics. An ARKANE Thriller Book 12
Copyright © J.F. Penn (2021). All rights reserved.

www.JFPenn.com

Paperback ISBN: 978-1-913321-82-6
Large Print ISBN: 978-1-913321-84-0
Hardback ISBN: 978-1-913321-83-3

Requests to publish work from this book
should be sent to: joanna@CurlUpPress.com

Cover and Interior Design: JD Smith Design

Printed by Amazon KDP Print

CURL UP
PRESS

www.CurlUpPress.com

PROLOGUE

Desert near Acre, the Holy Land. 1183.

DARK CLOUDS HID THE moon as the four knights rode out across desert scrub to the ruined temple in the Judean Hills. A blanket of night lay across the land, dulling all sound but their hoofbeats and a single far-off cry of a night bird. Crusaders had besieged the village that once surrounded the temple, the people slain or forced out under the banner of the scarlet cross. Only shadows remained now and perhaps the restless spirits of those who couldn't move on, but William de Tracy did not want to think of spirits tonight.

He looked up as a sliver of moonlight pierced the clouds and touched the edge of the ruined temple, turning the rough-hewn stone into the mottled silver of a blade. It had taken much blood and gold to uncover the ancient myth that surrounded this place, and William could only hope it would be worth it.

Twelve years fighting the heathen in this god-forsaken country.

Twelve years into a lifetime sentence for something he only did to serve his king.

Could this temple hold the key to ending their perdition?

Richard de Brito vaulted from his horse, leading the creature to the shadows as he tethered it at the side of the temple. Reginald FitzUrse and Hugh de Morville followed suit, but at a slower pace, both men suffering from battle wounds.

William's own movements were just as hampered, his body and soul exhausted from the penance of servitude, even as a knight here in the Holy Land. They had the privileges of rank, but they had no freedom to leave, banished by the Pope for their sins, their service the only way to buy a way into heaven.

In blazing days under the desert sun, William dreamed of England — the babbling brook at the edge of his estate, the dappled light of the forest, so gentle on the eyes compared to this savage land. It was holy to some, perhaps, but William would give it all to be home again.

"Are you sure this is the place, Will?" de Brito called out as he climbed over a low wall. "It looks to be only a ruin."

"And no doubt some Moor bastard has beaten us to whatever's left of the treasure." FitzUrse was bad-tempered at the best of times, but tonight, he seemed particularly out of sorts. His preferred squire had recently left and his armor was tarnished, his beard unkempt. The darkness that plagued them all hung over his head the most.

As de Morville helped his friend down, William dismounted, leaning gingerly on his left leg, a sword cut still healing on the limb. He would have considered it nothing in his younger days, but they were no longer knights of carefree summer. The memory of those years still held them together, but the bond of spilled blood remained their strongest tie. Without it, they would have gone their separate ways by now.

From his tunic William pulled a tattered map, a scrap of goatskin painted with intricate markings matted with dirt and hair that smelled of the grave. "This is the place. Before it was sacred to the Jews, it was an ancient burial ground. A place where those of myth were worshipped and where it's said, long life could be found."

William looked up from the map and into the labyrinth of broken pillars. "Come, we must be away before dawn."

The four knights picked their way through broken masonry, the destruction so complete that they were barely able to make out what once stood here. The air was still, as if something in the shadows held its breath, daring them to take another step.

The Crusaders had done their worst here, for sure, and the label of Crusader was one that William detested. It gathered all those who fought for Christ under one banner: the rabble of poor souls who begged at the roadside with empty bellies and the knight with jeweled armor and a feast awaiting him after battle. Both would meet God in heaven on the same terms, but down here, they would never be equals.

De Brito scrambled ahead until he disappeared into the darkness of a stone arch, still partially standing above the wreckage.

A minute later, he stuck his head back out. "Over here, there's a way down." He reached for an oil lamp and struck it alight, holding it high to illuminate the way ahead as they descended into darkness.

The stone steps were worn and slippery with the passage of feet over years, evidence of the life that once filled this place. It had echoed with the laughter of families, songs of praise to the Most High, and the weeping of mourners for the slaughtered. Now it was silent, and the scent of incense lingered under the damp mossy smell of water on stone as nature reclaimed what it had lost with each passing generation.

William let de Brito lead the way, aware of traps set for enthusiastic tomb raiders and keen for the younger man to set them off first. But no thud of stone on flesh came from ahead as they spiraled down into the earth, the circular staircase growing narrower as they descended.

This would be easy to defend, one way in and out, and no ability to see what was ahead. But William could sense no soldiers waiting in the dark. The bones of the dead were all that remained.

The air grew thin as they reached the bottom of the stairs and emerged into a vast circular tomb. There were niches around the sides, each one with a casket mounted within. These were not the body-sized coffins of English tombs, but boxes just big enough for long bones stacked beneath skulls after flesh had rotted away.

In the darkness, William stepped into a cobweb with viscous, thick strings that stuck to his face and quivered as he fought to escape. A huge spider with a bulbous body scuttled out of a hole in the stone. William thrust his arm up, slashing the web away, brushing it from his face as if to ward off the mark of the grave. He held up the torch to see more cobwebs coating every surface. A twitching layer, entwined with the hard stone, alive with the bodies of arachnids that spun their lives down here. Spiders that grew fat on the flesh of the dead.

William turned to look at the tomb. A deep pit lay in the center, edged with copper, engraved with words in Hebrew, Greek and Latin. FitzUrse picked up a fragment of masonry and dropped it down the hole. They stood listening for a moment, but there was no answering clunk, only a silence that spoke of the depths below.

"It would be better if we found decent plunder up here, old friend," FitzUrse grunted. "If it's down there, we'll have to find a scrawny infidel to retrieve it for us."

"Let's have a better look at this place." De Brito held his torch high and the flickering light played over a dusty scabbard encrusted with rubies. The reflection cast a crimson pall over the faces of the gathered men, and William had a sense that they were all bathed in tainted blood.

they left Rome — and he had no intention of sharing it with them.

The Pope was old and sick and the many relics laid upon his body brought no relief while the prayers of the faithful did nothing to ease his pain. The Pope had legitimized forced conversion of heathens and promised remission of sin for fighting in the Crusades, but he had so much more to do to fulfill his mission on earth.

That night, Pope Alexander had told William of a fabled relic, the heart of Methuselah, who lived for nearly a thousand years. It promised the miracle of long life and if he brought it to Rome, William would be absolved of his sins. More than that, he would be honored with high office and reunited with his family.

He could return to England.

The relic was his way back and the longing for home drove William onward. They plundered tomb after tomb until, finally, he discovered the map to this one.

He bent to examine the casket more closely. It was carved from walnut wood, but the whorls once polished to a fine grain were now covered in cobwebs and the dust of ages. William brushed the casket clean with the hem of his cloak to reveal what lay beneath. Etched Latin words next to Greek, Hebrew, and what looked like images of ancient Egyptian hieroglyphics. Perhaps the same phrase repeated in each language to make sure the meaning was clear. William could read the Latin and Greek.

From death comes life. Life is the price.

He frowned. Surely life was the reward?

He opened the casket. The hinges squeaked a little, stiff with rust and lack of use. Inside lay a shriveled organ, blackened with time, a desiccated heart resting upon a piece of folded parchment. William glanced back at the others. They were busy stuffing bags full of relic boxes, raiding each niche for valuables, bundling up precious items with cobwebs and dust to sift out what could be sold on later.

But this tomb of relics held only one real treasure.

William pushed down the dark foreboding that rose inside, pulled off his glove and reached out a finger.

He touched the heart. It was strangely warm, even in the chill of the tomb.

It pulsed suddenly with a double beat.

William jerked back with a quick intake of breath. He looked around to see if the others had noticed, but they were engrossed in their plunder and paid him no heed.

He reached out once more and laid his fingertips on the organ.

It pulsed again.

William frowned as he considered what it might mean. Other relics were mere pieces of dead flesh, but this was clearly something far more. If the Pope wanted it, then it was precious indeed.

Unseen by the others, William wrapped the heart in the parchment it lay upon and slipped both inside his tunic, next to his skin. He placed the box in his bag and joined the others in ransacking the surrounding niches. They would have a rich haul tonight, enough to buy them many months of luxury in the Holy Land. Enough to satisfy the others so they did not question what he withheld.

As the four knights left the tomb, now relieved of all its relics, William felt the heart pulse next to his own, a promise of life in every beat.

Perhaps he would not take it to Rome after all…

CHAPTER 1

Canterbury, England

IT WAS EARLY MORNING as Morgan Sierra walked
through the streets, navigating puddles from last night's rain
that reflected the pale blue sky above. Her dark curls were
tucked into a woolen beanie and she thrust her hands deep
into her pockets, huddling up in her fleece jacket against the
chill. It was quiet, even though the cathedral precinct lay in
the center of the city's shopping area. British people were not
early risers, especially in the depths of winter.

Director Marietti had called late last night about a theft
from the cathedral, one that needed to be kept quiet. A
simple theft didn't seem like a mission for ARKANE, but
after her years as an agent, Morgan knew things were often
more complex than they seemed at first.

The Arcane Religious Knowledge And Numinous Experience (ARKANE) Institute investigated supernatural mysteries around the world. They focused on relics of power,
religious and occult forces, and threats that verged on the
supernatural. Her ARKANE partner, Jake Timber, was away
on another case, but if needed, he would join her. She would
assess what was going on first. Marietti had provided little

insight, but it was a chance to see one of the country's most famous cathedrals and that was worth a trip.

Morgan arrived at the imposing Christchurch Gate that led into the Canterbury Cathedral precinct. It brought to mind the entrance of a castle with two stone turrets and crenellations between, where archers could lean over to fire down on invaders. A bronze statue of Christ in Glory sat in the center flanked by stone carvings — the arms of the Tudor dynasty, heraldic symbols, and angels with outstretched wings. A huge arch surrounded a thick, oversized wooden door next to a smaller entrance, just big enough to step through. It had a bell mounted beside it, an out-of-place modern juxtaposition to the medieval grandeur of the gate.

Morgan pressed the bell and moments later, a young police constable opened the wooden door, her black uniform freshly pressed, her peaked cap marked with blue and white checks and the badge of the cathedral in the center.

"Morning, Ms Sierra," the constable said. "The Dean told us you were coming."

Morgan stepped through the gate. "Thank you for letting me in so early. I didn't know the cathedral had its own police."

The constable led the way into the precinct at a quick pace. "Yes, this is our patch. The custom goes back to the twelfth century, so we have a long pedigree."

As they walked across the courtyard, the smell of coffee wafted out from the tiny office by the door. Morgan really wanted to ask for a cup, but the constable seemed to be in a hurry. A theft on the grounds would usually be their jurisdiction, so perhaps her presence wasn't wanted — or perhaps the constabulary didn't know of the theft as yet. Marietti said to speak only with the Dean about the situation.

Morgan looked up at the imposing cathedral as they walked through the grounds. Founded in the sixth century, it had been rebuilt in medieval times and expanded into the

Gothic style. Primarily constructed of Caen limestone, the upper tower gleamed with golden light in the rising dawn, a truly magnificent site for weary pilgrims and inspiring awe in the faithful. But extensive renovation work currently shrouded the true grandeur of the cathedral. Scaffolding cloaked one tower like a metal skin and giant wooden boards stood around the base of the building telling the story of the renovation. They portrayed images of those who worked upon stone and stained glass, as well as listing the manuscripts and artifacts inside, some of which pre-dated even the cathedral.

As much as she would have liked to see the building in all its glory, Morgan felt privileged to witness the cathedral this way. Stonemasons worked here now as they had done for over a thousand years, an ancient craft passed down through family ties and apprenticeships. The work they did with their hands and traditional tools gave the cathedral hundreds more years of life, and generations to come would look upon their carvings.

Much of the renovation fought against the inevitable process of entropy, the gradual decline into disorder that happened to everything in life. The artisans only replaced parts of the building when it was absolutely necessary, choosing to restore rather than rebuild in most cases. It was slow and painstaking, the work of a generation and a poignant reminder of the brevity of human life against the backdrop of history.

Morgan accepted that everything she did would disappear, that no one would remember the missions where she and Jake risked everything, that their actions were ultimately ephemeral. But when they passed on, these stones would remain — and that was a kind of comfort.

Tiers of niches flanked the arched entranceway into the cathedral, each containing a statue of a notable person in Church history. Amongst them, Morgan could make out the medieval Archbishop Anselm, and Thomas Cranmer, leader of the English Reformation, burned at the stake in 1556. Unusually, there was also a female figure, St Bertha, a sixth-century queen of Kent, whose Christian influence helped to spread the faith across pagan England.

There were fifty-five statues around the entranceway, but two new figures stood out in particular from the weathered stone. Queen Elizabeth II and the Duke of Edinburgh, their mature features carved with care. The British monarch was the Supreme Governor of the Church of England, but Morgan wondered whether this Queen would be the last honored here. The popularity of the monarchy waned in these modern times, but then again, the cathedral was testament to the longevity of tradition against the tide of history. Time answered all questions, solved all conflicts, and these stones had witnessed much in over a thousand years of faith.

The constable opened the door and gestured for Morgan to enter. "The Dean is waiting near the altar."

Morgan walked into the shadowed nave, her footsteps echoing on the stone floor. A single ray of sunlight lanced through one of the high arched windows and illuminated slender pillars rising to the vault above. The nave was set with modern chairs, much easier to move around than the wooden pews so often found in English churches.

After the glimpse of wild nature in the hunt for the Tree of Life on her last mission, Morgan appreciated this architectural order. There was beauty in the stark lines of stone pillars and soaring arches, and in the carvings made by skilled artisans. Yet, even as she stood in this sacred place, the air dense with a millennium of prayers offered by the faithful, disquiet edged into her mind. The chill of winter seemed more intense here, as if the stone amplified the cold and sucked warmth from her body.

She walked further in. A lone figure knelt on the flagstones in front of a plain altar, head bent in prayer, dwarfed by the grandeur of the surrounding cathedral. Morgan hung back, waiting for the Dean to finish.

Before the Reformation, this had been a Catholic cathedral, but now it was the seat of the Archbishop of the Church of England. There were no bloody crucifixes or icons of tortured saints. Only an altar covered with a white cloth, and topped with a plain cross. An ornate Victorian pulpit stood against a pillar to one side, its colored imagery of the crucifixion and annunciation a contrast to the surrounding stark stone.

A compass rose lay inset into the flagstones before the altar, a symbol of Anglican Communion worldwide, engraved with Greek words from the New Testament. "The truth will set you free." Morgan recognized the text from the book of John, chapter eight. But whose truth, she wondered — and not for the first time.

The Dean stood up from prayer and turned to greet her. He was a tall, angular man with tightly cropped white hair that stood out against his black skin. Deep laughter lines crinkled around his eyes and as he smiled, Morgan couldn't help but respond in kind. If only all clergy were so inviting. His warmth radiated in the frosty morning, but she also sensed an underlying anxiety.

"Good morning. You must be Morgan Sierra. Welcome to our cathedral."

"Thank you, I wish I had more time to look around but Director Marietti said you had an urgent problem."

The Dean's smile faded and his lanky frame, relaxed just a moment before, became taut and stiff. "Yes, come. I'll show you."

He led Morgan behind the simple altar to the crossing, a raised area where the nave intersected with the transept. It lay in front of the pulpitum, a large stone screen that separated the choir area from the rest of the church, and Morgan couldn't help but stop to look at the detail. A wide stone archway flanked by statues of kings with angels above, all surrounded by intricate carvings that mirrored the tall columns in the nave.

"It was built in 1450," the Dean said, noting her interest. "Back in Catholic times, only members of the priory could cross into the space beyond. Of course, we believe there is no separation between us and our Father in heaven, no need for intercession by those ordained. Anyone can speak to God and read His Word."

Morgan reflected on the similarities to the Holy of Holies in the ancient Jewish Temple, the place where God dwelt and only priests could enter. This cathedral was certainly an interesting mix of Catholic history and architecture with a modern faith that used a simple altar in the nave, and kept the high altar beyond for feast days and special occasions.

"It's always good to meet another fan of Gothic architecture," the Dean continued, the warm smile returning to his face as he noted her expression. "And sometimes eyes like yours mean you see the world differently, perhaps even into realms the rest of us cannot perceive. Do you find that to be true?"

Morgan's cobalt blue eyes were indeed distinctive, with a slash of violet through the right. Her twin sister Faye had the same slash through the opposite eye, and they certainly saw things differently. In recent years, they had become closer because of Morgan's clear devotion to her little niece Gemma. Faye had been raised by their Christian mother in England, while Morgan had been brought up in Israel by their Jewish father. A family torn apart by faith and geography was not so uncommon in this multicultural age, but perhaps she did see things differently because of her mixed upbringing. Her missions with ARKANE had certainly opened her eyes to more.

Morgan nodded. "I'm not sure whether it's a gift or a curse."

The Dean put a gentle hand on her arm. "Sometimes that does not become clear until we reach the end of things. Only time can provide wisdom. Until then, we have faith to guide us."

He indicated a chapel to the side of the crossing. "This way."

As they walked on, a meow came from the shadows, and a small grey cat darted out. It wound its way between the Dean's legs and he bent to stroke it.

"You shouldn't be in here, Willow." As his face transformed from authoritative clergyman to cat lover, Morgan couldn't help but smile at the obvious bond between the two.

She thought of her own cat, Shmi, back in her little house in Jericho, Oxford. He pretty much lived with her old neighbor down the street these days, returning occasionally when Morgan was briefly home between missions. She hunkered down to stroke Willow, enjoying the feel of her soft fur.

"You're a cat person, too." The Dean nodded with an approving smile. "Willow lives in the rectory, but she gets a lot of attention in here, so she's often around the place. Come, we must hurry before the other clergy arrive."

They descended a small flight of stairs into a side chapel with Gothic archways and carvings similar to the rest of the cathedral. In such a grand building, this small chapel should have been unremarkable — but it had a unique, historical resonance.

A metal cross flanked by two jagged swords hung above a plain grey marble altar. Light from the high windows above cast shadows behind the swords, so there appeared to be four blades pointing down to the sacred place where blood was spilled on holy ground over 850 years ago.

"This is the Martyrdom site of Archbishop Thomas Becket," the Dean said. "And the scene of the crime I need you to investigate."

CHAPTER 2

Breton Biomedical, Boston, USA

It didn't take very long to dismember a human body, especially if you knew which parts were valuable and should be extracted carefully and which could be disassembled more quickly.

Dr. Kelley Montague-Breton made her first incision as the clock ticked past two a.m. Her slender hands were deft and confident in white medical gloves that covered her pale, freckled skin and her abundance of strawberry blonde curls lay tucked up inside a medical cap. Her face was freshly cleaned of the precise makeup she wore during the day as armor against the corporate world in the towering offices above. Down here in the levels below ground, Kelley could strip back to essentials. The dead didn't judge and there was no one to witness her at this time of night.

She wore blue scrubs that hung loose over her slender frame. Naturally petite, Kelley knew she was too thin at the moment, a result of anxiety that gnawed at her gut and kept her from sleep most nights. Nightmares punctuated the few fitful hours she managed — and the sense of dread continued to haunt her days.

Kelley rarely processed corpses herself these days. As CEO of Breton Biomedical, she had an entire team of disarticulators to do the grunt work. But disassembly took her mind off everything else. She could focus on each cut of the blade, each rasp of the saw.

Full tissue recovery was labor intensive, but she would start the process and her team could finish the job later. No part of the precious human body would be left unused. It was an anatomy jigsaw puzzle in reverse as she removed each separate part, complicated enough to keep her attention on the task and not on the email that had come through yesterday afternoon.

The disassembly room was a hybrid space, somewhere between a morgue and an operating theatre with clinical white tiles and stainless steel equipment. Metal trolleys on rolling wheels flanked each side of the room with vats of preserving liquid and sterile storage boxes ready for the parts that would be dispersed after processing. It smelled of strong disinfectant, and air conditioning kept the room at a few degrees below a comfortable working temperature. There was no need for beeping equipment monitoring signs of life — the cadaver on the metal gurney had no need of them.

The man's pectoral muscles were firm under Kelley's gloved hand as she cut into his flesh, an intimacy that no living lover could have experienced. He had a scar on his chest, a sunburst of tissue, but the story behind it was now only a memory for those he left behind. As she sliced, Kelley focused on the rhythm of her breath, the quiet tick of the clock, the puff of airflow through the room. For these few mindful hours, she could forget everything else.

Her father had taught her the methods of disassembly during Kelley's teenage years. A strange bond perhaps, but one she appreciated. Both of them preferred the quiet of disarticulation to the boardroom meetings and etiquette of business that kept the wheels turning and the money pouring in. As an only child, Kelley inherited the company on her father's death — as well as its secrets. But she was intent on being the last Breton to shoulder this burden of generations.

Neither of her two sons were interested in joining the firm and she intended that they live out the lives they chose. But there was much to be done to keep the curse of knowledge from them and Kelley could only hope she would have the strength to complete what must be done before it was too late.

She looked down at the body before her, a particularly valuable corpse. A Caucasian man in his early forties, naked on the slab, with a square of gauze over his face to preserve some sense of dignity. Not that there could ever be much dignity in death, when a human was reduced to a pile of meat, with nothing of the real person left behind.

This man had the body of someone who worked out regularly and looked after his diet. Shame about the massive heart attack that killed him, possibly from some genetic defect that no amount of lifestyle change could avoid. But the rest of him would help many others — and the bottom line of her company.

It was illegal to pay for corpses or body parts in the USA, and the National Organ Transplant Act and the Uniform Anatomical Gift Act prevented profit from the sale of organs, particularly if used in human transplantation. The business in corpses was payment for 'processing,' a service fee for the time and labor to harvest each part, as well as the further use of what remained.

The postmortem biomaterials industry was a necessary one, hidden under technical terms that made it easy to forget there were actual human bodies involved. A basic corpse might be worth thirty- to fifty-thousand dollars, but they could fetch over two hundred thousand once processed into products like demineralized bone matrices, medical implants or skin grafts. Most people didn't know and, in fact, didn't want to know about the necroeconomy that lay beneath aspects of health care. They just wanted their pain to stop and another day alive in the world.

While there were rumors of a 'red market' for whole cadavers, organs and bones from developing markets, Breton Biomedical worked with a trusted body broker to avoid the potential of using corpses without consent. That had taken other biomedical companies under in the past and Kelley would not have it destroy what her family had worked so hard to build over generations.

She would do that on her own terms.

With a sigh she considered the necessary trip ahead. Back to the place that lay behind her sleepless nights and the dark shadows under her eyes. She could face a boardroom of corporate lawyers or a pack of vitriolic press reporters with a backbone of steel, but what awaited her in England brought her out in a cold sweat.

Kelley refocused on the task at hand, each slice of the scalpel anchoring her to the present moment. This man's corpse would help countless others without suffering for his donation.

From death comes life. It was the motto of the company, although few knew that the Latin version, *Ex morte vita,* was carved upon her ancestral family coat of arms back in England on the estate she avoided as much as possible.

Kelley sliced away the remaining ligaments and underly-ing muscle around the neck, tightened the brace that held the head immobile, and picked up the bone saw. This head was promised to a training school for plastic surgeons who paid handsomely for the labor to process it so they could practice the operations that made them rich.

The physical work of sawing through bone made her sweat a little, even in the cold room. The sound was rhyth-mic, almost hypnotic, but underneath, Kelley sensed the savagery of dismemberment. It was a violent act to saw the head from another human being and for a moment she imagined the features of another underneath the square of gauze.

A decomposing face with pinches of skin stitched together in a macabre patchwork. Eyes of piercing turquoise, like Egyptian jewels laid out upon the dead.

Kelley imagined those eyes opening and the smell of rot and decaying flesh filling the room. She shuddered and pushed the image away, focusing back on the task at hand as the memory of the stench faded.

After removing the head, Kelley began the painstaking process of harvesting large swatches of skin from the man's torso. Sold by the gram, skin was an incredibly precious resource. Cadaver repurposing did not cross any legal or moral lines, but Kelley understood that next of kin expectations rarely matched the reality. Did this man's family know that his body lay in the disassembly room while they were mired in the throes of grief?

But such was the natural order of things.

Her father had always said there was no point in fighting death. It would always win in the end. Time ticked forward and you could not stop the clock.

Their business was built on pushing back the point at which it claimed another life, an attempt to keep the spark of light alive for another month, another year. Her father had lain upon this slab — although Kelley had left his disassembly to others — and she would lie here too one day. She only hoped she could free her sons from their family's cursed history before then.

She sliced once more and eased back the skin from the man's chest. It was a delicate task, as each segment of cadaver skin needed to be kept intact. The size of the piece determined its possible usage and the corpse of an adult could provide four to six square feet from the flat surfaces of chest, back and thighs. Large jars of saline solution infused with antibiotics stood on trolleys beside the gurney where the skin would be stored for refrigeration and used within a few weeks. Some would be freeze-dried and turned into biological wound dressings, packaged in foil pouches with rehydration instructions for the military. Clear biohazard markings distinguished it from dehydrated field ration kits that apparently looked disturbingly similar.

The defense contract was one of their most lucrative and also one that Kelley was personally proud of. Those who served their country deserved the best medical care and, while there were many things wrong with the way veterans were treated, at least their skin grafts were of good quality.

As she placed the square of skin in a jar, she wondered where this piece would end up. As much as she hoped it would go to some deserving veteran, it could just as easily be used in bladder incontinence surgery, eyelid reconstruction, or other dermal fillers for those who could not live with what nature gave them.

As Kelley gently placed the final swatch of skin in pre-serving fluid, she sighed once more. Time was running out. She couldn't put off the trip to England any longer.

CHAPTER 3

Canterbury, England

MORGAN WALKED FORWARD TO look more closely at the Martyrdom site. Copper candlesticks stood on either side of an altar topped with thick white candles, lit with a steady flame. A wooden rail with a kneeling cushion welcomed devoted pilgrims to prayer and red letters on the stone spelled out the name of the saint, as crimson as Becket's blood when it was spilled on this holy ground.

She knew the history of England's most famous Catholic saint, cut down by four knights in 1170 after rash words by King Henry II and canonized soon after. In previous missions, she and Jake had recovered powerful relics of the early Church, physical remains of saints that some believed had supernatural powers. But there should be no relics in an Anglican church. This cathedral hadn't been Catholic since the sixteenth century and given the bloody history between Christian denominations, it was surprising to find even an altar for Becket.

Morgan frowned as she turned back to the Dean. "So what was stolen?"

He pointed at a carved wooden plinth topped with a

glass case to one side of the altar. A clear indentation lay in the center of the red velvet lining and a precise circular hole was visible in the glass.

The case was empty.

"The Becket reliquary was taken sometime in the night." The Dean pulled out his phone and swiped to a photo, enlarging the image before handing it to Morgan.

The reliquary was the size of a large brooch, a silver oval with decorative filigree edges, and a window of glass. A fragment of bone lay inside, wrapped in red velvet and secured with golden thread. A Latin inscription ran around the outside: *Ex Cranio St Thomae Cantvariensis.* From the skull of St Thomas of Canterbury.

"The reliquary has been safe in Liège, Belgium for many years," the Dean explained. "It was brought here for an inter-faith ceremony, the most important in many years." He fell silent for a moment. In the stillness of the cathedral, there was no sound but their breathing.

The Dean bent closer and spoke softly. "His Holiness, Pope Francis, is coming and will pray here at the altar. It's critical that we get it back before he arrives in five days." He wrung his hands together. "Word of this theft could jeopardize the ceremony, which is why I called Director Marietti. Our friendship goes back many years and I know ARKANE has experience in such matters."

"But why not involve the constabulary on the grounds or use the Vatican's resources?" Morgan asked.

The Dean pointed to a stone plaque on the wall to one side.

In this place hallowed by the martyrdom of Thomas Becket 29 December 1170, Pope John Paul II and Robert Runcie, Archbishop of Canterbury, knelt together in prayer 29 May 1982.

"The conflict between our Church and the Catholics goes back to the Reformation, the Dissolution of the Monasteries, and the many wars that have been fought since." The Dean paced the chapel, his expression troubled. "That visit by Pope John Paul II was the first ever by a reigning Pope. Pope Benedict XVI came in 2010, but you must know of the controversies surrounding his papacy."

Morgan nodded. The German Joseph Ratzinger, who later became Pope Benedict XVI, had been a member of Hitler Youth as was legally required of men his age. He was drafted into the German Army and served before becoming a priest. While many accepted that aspect of his past, Morgan's father and many other Jews had never forgiven his support for the beatification of Pope Pius XII, who stayed silent as millions were sent to the concentration camps.

The Dean continued. "Pope Francis is loved by many outside the Catholic Church for his humility and dedication to the poor. Given the state of the world right now, this interfaith celebration is much needed. Of course, Anglicans don't value relics in a religious sense. We only need God's Word and the power of prayer. But the relic of the martyrdom is precious to those attending, so we must get it back."

Morgan examined the empty glass case on the plinth. "It must have been a professional job, since you have so much security on the grounds. Do you have camera footage?"

The Dean shook his head, worry lines deepening on his brow. "The renovations are ongoing and yesterday, a block of stone fell and damaged the cable to the cameras. We have nothing for the last twenty-four hours. The constabulary officers are working to restore it."

Morgan raised an eyebrow as she walked around the plinth. "The timing of the accident seems fortuitous. Was anything else taken?"

"No, only this."

The sound of running feet came from the nave.

A moment later, a choirboy burst into the chapel, his white robe tangling around his legs as he rushed in, eyes wide, cheeks flushed.

"You must come, Dean." His voice was loud with excitement and echoed around the chapel, the sound almost shocking after the quiet contemplation of the Martyrdom. "There's something you need to see."

The Dean reached out a hand. "Hush now, what is it?"

"This way."

Morgan and the Dean followed the boy back out of the chapel and into the choir stalls where ranks of Victorian wooden benches allowed the full number of singers: twelve adult Lay Clerks, and twenty-five choristers.

The choirboy ran between two of the benches and pointed to something on a red-cushioned seat. "Here. I didn't want to touch it."

The Dean edged his way in between the seats and smiled at the discovery. He bent down and gently picked up the reliquary. "Praise God. The thief must have dropped it. Perhaps someone startled them."

His tone expressed a deep gratitude for the gift of the returned relic, but Morgan felt a shiver of unease. Something wasn't right here.

"Thank you." The Dean nodded at the choirboy. "Back to your study now, and no word of this to the others."

The boy smiled and walked off with a spring in his step at the secret discovery.

The Dean cupped the reliquary in his palm and bowed his head toward the altar, praying in silence for a minute before turning to Morgan.

"It seems I brought you here for no reason after all, but at least I can offer you a coffee after we put this back."

As much as Morgan really needed a hit of caffeine, the sudden discovery of the reliquary bothered her. It was too much of a coincidence, but then her ARKANE missions had made her pretty sensitive to the mysteries of relics. Perhaps it was nothing. Perhaps she just needed that coffee.

As the Dean led her back toward the chapel, Morgan

noticed an unusual cadaver tomb on one side of the altar surrounded by a colorful arch and decorated with figures from the Church. While most tombs in the cathedral were grand monuments commemorating the life of the dead, this tomb was quite different. It had two levels, almost like a bunk bed. The effigy of an Archbishop in full ecclesiastical robes and gold mitre lay on top. His skin was painted as fresh as it had been in life and it looked as if he could rise and lead a service. Directly underneath lay a statue of the Archbishop's cadaver, grey skin tight against his skeleton, naked except for a shroud. Stripped of his finery, the Archbishop was just another human body ready for the grave.

The Dean noticed her interest. "Archbishop Henry Chichele died in 1443, but he had this built while he was alive and stared down at it as he preached. He believed it was important to remember death while still living. No matter our status in life, we all end up the same way."

"*Memento mori*, indeed," Morgan said softly, considering how many others had considered the brevity of life in this very spot over hundreds of years.

The cadaver effigy of the Archbishop with his tonsured head was also a reminder that Becket's physical body had lain in this place after his brutal murder. Morgan glanced down at the reliquary in the Dean's cupped hands. Was the fragment of skull inside really Becket's? Did it matter if it wasn't? She supposed it mattered to some, but perhaps it was faith that gave the object its power, not something intrinsic within the bone.

Morgan looked once more at the face of the cadaver effigy and then followed the Dean to the chapel of the Martyrdom.

The sacred space had a sense of expectation, as if the ghosts of the faithful held their breath as they waited for the relic to be restored. The Dean laid the reliquary back inside the glass box, resting it gently into the red velvet indentation.

He pulled out his phone as he walked around to look at it

from the front once more. "I'll call the glazier right now and stay here until he arrives. The security cameras will be back on today and all will be right once more."

He frowned and leaned forward to look more closely at the jewel. "I've stared at this for so long over the last week that I know each filigree element intricately. I've counted every gold stitch as I prayed here for the guidance of God to be as faithful as Becket."

The Dean looked over at Morgan, his dark eyes desolate. "This isn't the same reliquary. This is a fake. So where is the genuine relic of Saint Thomas?"

CHAPTER 4

As the bells chimed eleven, Morgan emerged from the nave and walked around the outside of the cathedral toward the ruins of the abbey of St Augustine. Elegant stone arches were all that remained of the infirmary chapel, but she found the stark beauty of the architecture more conducive to quiet contemplation than the grand cathedral now in the throes of another busy day.

The sky above was a pale grey and, although the sun tried to pierce the heavy clouds, the chill of winter still crept in through her fleece jacket. Morgan sat on a block of stone amongst a tangle of wild ivy, the smell of crushed foliage mingling with the scent of herbs from the border garden just beyond the ruins. Lichen grew on the stone in shades of mottled mustard and lime green, evidence that nature would always claim back its domain. No matter how many times people built upon the earth, eventually, it would all crumble to ruin. *Memento mori* was not only a reminder that each person would die, but also that every edifice created by humanity would eventually turn to dust.

Morgan thought back to the last mission to find the Tree of Life. In the depths of a holy mountain, she had glimpsed a possible future where untamed nature took back the earth. It had a form of savage beauty, but there was no place for the unique creativity of humans, who could imagine such a place as this cathedral and will it into being. She preferred to live in a world where both co-existed, even when it meant a constant struggle for equilibrium.

Her phone buzzed with a message. *I'm here.*

Morgan emerged from the ruins and spotted Martin Klein standing at the back gate of the cathedral grounds accompanied by a police constable. Martin wore a purple backpack over a bright red raincoat and, with his shock of messy blonde hair and wire-rimmed glasses, he looked like an overgrown schoolboy arriving eagerly for his first day. But Martin's youthful appearance belied his true ability to discover hidden patterns in data and manipulate the digital world in a way that Morgan and other agents had come to rely on.

He was the Head Librarian and Archivist of ARKANE, unofficially known as the Brain of the Institute, responsible for the powerhouse of knowledge that drove their missions. Over the years, agents had retrieved ancient manuscripts and occult texts, medieval books and forbidden artifacts. Martin had scanned each one to add to his ever increasing web of data, ensuring that ARKANE agents could find what they needed to stop evil when it emerged.

Martin waved as he caught sight of her and the constable let him through. Morgan met him halfway across the fore-court in front of the War Horse, an oversized statue made of wooden fragments commemorating the eight million horses killed during the First World War.

Morgan stood back a little, respecting Martin's need for personal space as he bobbed up and down on the balls of his feet, his words running over one another in his haste to get started.

"The picture of the relic you sent over. It's an important reliquary, created around 1666 and held by the British Jesuit Province in Liège, Belgium, where there was a school for Catholic education. It moved to Stonyhurst College in England in 1794 and—"

"Let's walk and talk," Morgan said softly and headed back along the path toward the side door of the cathedral as Martin continued.

"Stonyhurst has an interesting set of relics including those of Becket, forty English martyrs, and even a thorn from the Crown of Thorns owned by Mary, Queen of Scots, who was, of course, beheaded by Queen Elizabeth I." He sighed. "These relics have such a bloody history."

Further along the path, they passed a large block of stone carved with the figure of a pilgrim, a pack on his back and a staff in his hand. Letters spelled out *Via Francigena* around him, marking the beginning of the pilgrimage from Canterbury across Europe to Rome.

Morgan considered how it might feel to walk away with only a pack on her back, to leave all this behind and focus on one step after another along the two thousand kilometers to the heart of the Catholic Church. A smile played on her lips as she considered the freedom that might bring, but as Martin walked into the cathedral in front of her, she pushed the idea away. There would be time for such things when she tired of ARKANE missions, but right now, they had a mystery to solve and Morgan sensed this was no ordinary theft.

She led Martin to the chapel of the Martyrdom where he wasted no time in unloading the backpack and setting up his equipment. The Dean stood at the entranceway to make sure no one witnessed their actions, maintaining the guise that the genuine relic remained in place.

Martin placed the reliquary onto a small metal plate, similar to kitchen scales but packed with sensors, then swept another handheld device over it.

"This checks the age of the surrounding metal and can penetrate inside the reliquary to the bone," he explained.

Morgan watched in silence. It was better to let Martin do his thing and wait for his conclusions before asking questions. They had worked together in the field several times and he always had valuable insights, although his actions had put him in danger in the past and she worried about him as a sister might for a wayward brother.

A few minutes later, Martin finished scanning and tapped on his laptop as he processed the results. "I built these models for artifacts brought back for the vault. They are pretty accurate in finding fakes and I've discovered quite a few over the years."

The machine beeped twice, and Martin sighed. "And this is, in fact, a fake. A beautiful object, for sure, but definitely a forgery."

The machine beeped again, and he leaned in to examine the results more carefully. "Now that is interesting. There are chemical and mineralogical signatures in gold that can trace the batch. This one matches a relic held in the Basilica of St Mary in Kraków, Poland." He frowned. "The bone matches too, even though the relic in St Mary's is meant to be Saint Stanislaus. But this bone is only around fifty years old. It's from a recent corpse, not a medieval saint."

As she considered his words, Morgan gazed at the reliquary, wondering whose bone lay within and how it had been harvested. Perhaps the answer lay in Kraków.

* * *

Kraków, Poland

Later that afternoon, Morgan stood in the market square in front of the Bazylika Mariacka, the Catholic Basilica of St Mary at the heart of Stare Miasto, the historical part of the city. She sipped a black coffee as she waited for Jake Timber, her ARKANE partner who was flying in separately from Vienna.

The basilica was red brick in the Polish Gothic style. It had two spires, one towering over the other, with a crown above a host of smaller turrets like a miniature castle. Arched windows interspersed the brick with touches of white, and above the main doors, a statue of Mary gazed down to bless the faithful as they entered to worship.

The market traders in the square were packing up for the day, filling boxes with leftover goods and shouting last-minute deals to the tourists who wandered around as locals hurried home after work.

Kraków was only a few hours' flight from London, but the Polish language and the different architecture were a reminder that she was a long way from Canterbury, where Morgan had started the day. One of the beauties of Europe was how close everything was, how different cultures over-laid each other in dense historical layers that echoed into the present.

But that was also its danger.

Kraków was just over an hour's drive from Auschwitz-Birkenau where over a million Jews were murdered in the concentration camp, along with hundreds of thousands of gays, Roma and others unwanted by the Third Reich. Three million Polish Jews were exterminated during those dark days, estimated to be ninety percent of Jews in the country.

Poland had once been considered the most tolerant country in Europe when it came to religion, and a principal cultural center, home to one of the largest Jewish populations in the world. After the Holocaust, some Jews had returned, but many still fought for property rights as the government considered them to be citizens of pre-war Poland and not necessarily due restitution.

Morgan had experienced the rise of European anti-Semitism personally during her time in Budapest, when she fought alongside Jews at the Dohány Street Synagogue as the mob descended. She could only hope sense would prevail here and Ashkenazi Jews could build their culture once more upon the ashes of the lost.

A trumpet sounded from the tower, the *hejnal mariacki*, played every hour of every day of the year. The plaintive tune cut off mid-song to commemorate the trumpeter shot in the throat while sounding the alarm as Mongols attacked the city in the thirteenth century.

Morgan considered how strange it was to commemorate such a thing, while the country turned a blind eye to injustice happening in the present. But then chasing history was part of her job at ARKANE. The deeds of the past echoed through time and its ripples expanded into the present.

Jake was off chasing down such a mystery in Vienna, and although it was good for them to work on different things, Morgan missed him when he was away. Their relationship was complicated, but she trusted Jake to have her back and his skills complemented her own. They had both made mistakes on missions; they had both been damaged in body and spirit, but those experiences only brought them closer.

Much as she sometimes considered the possibility of taking things further, Morgan understood the dangers of becoming involved with someone who loved the knife-edge of risk and who flirted with death on a regular basis. She had been married once, back in the Israel Defense Force, but her husband Elian had died in a hail of bullets on the Golan Heights and his death crippled her for a time. Having left Israel to start a new life in Oxford, she met Jake on her first ARKANE mission to find the Pentecost stones. Life turns on these sudden moments — and bullets were perhaps the most sudden of all.

"Enjoying the view?"

Morgan spun around at Jake's voice and smiled to see him approach, backpack slung over one muscled shoulder, wearing a tan leather jacket that had seen better days.

"How was Vienna?"

"Not over yet, and I might need your help, but Marietti said this was urgent." Jake raised his left eyebrow, the faint corkscrew scar twisting up to his hairline as he frowned. "Something about the Pope and a missing relic?"

Morgan explained the details as they walked across the square to the doors of St Mary's. It was dark in the entrance hall, but then the space opened up into something quite extraordinary.

"If there had been no Rome, Kraków would indeed have been Rome," Morgan murmured the words first spoken by Giovanni Mucante, papal legate to Kraków in the sixteenth century. Now she could see why he spoke so highly of the city.

CHAPTER 5

As the *HEJNAL MARIACKI* echoed across the rooftops, Henry Palarae didn't even look up. It was merely another note in the soundscape of the city that marked the passage of time, but Henry worked on unique objects that would last far beyond the lifetime of the trumpet player, far beyond even his own life. Flesh and blood, skin and sinew rotted away, but bone and precious metal remained. Henry's only goal was to ensure his work survived many more lifetimes than his own.

He sat in the office at the back of his jeweler's shop surrounded by bookshelves, sketching a design for a brooch onto thick cream paper. There were still a few tourists wandering outside on the cobbled street, but he would hear the doorbell if any entered to peruse his religious artifacts. He snatched every moment to work on his creations, his hand moving swiftly over the page with the mechanical pencil he used for all his drafting. Some artisans had switched to designing on tablets with a digital stylus, but Henry loved the connection between lead and paper, his lines sweeping across the smooth texture of the blank page as a new creation emerged.

He bit his lip as he finished the brooch and turned to a fresh page in the sketchbook, sensing the glimmer of an idea that he couldn't quite translate into tangible form yet. Something swirling around the arrow-pierced torso of Saint Sebastian.

But there was no need to rush it.

Henry trusted the emergence of creativity. Something would spark the idea into life, he was sure of it, and in the meantime, he had plenty of less ambitious work to do.

The Palarae shop was small but opulent with carefully chosen religious pieces displayed to enhance their value. A detailed miniature of the Virgin Mary in a gold oval frame dotted with pearls. An ornate crucifix made from silver stolen from Jews during the Second World War, inlaid with tiny rubies representing droplets of the blood of Christ. Glass fronted display cases contained smaller pieces: religious medals, crucifixes and rosaries that honored God in a more affordable way.

An incense burner in the corner filled the air with the same scent as the basilica. It helped remind the faithful why they came to the shop in the first place and also masked the smell of damp that persisted in the medieval quarter.

The Basilica of St Mary inspired much of Henry's art and he appreciated the God of the Catholics, who reveled in blood and suffering. At least He seemed to, judging by the glorification of such things in the extravagant art of the church. More importantly, the religious liked to spend on beautiful objects and Henry served that need every day.

The jeweler's shop was just one level of this old house in the medieval heart of Stare Miasto, where artisans had worked on their craft for generations. Several floors of rooms formed the living quarters above, mostly unused since he was an only son with no family of his own. His mother was usually ensconced in the uppermost flat, closest to God. If only He would hurry up and take her. But she mostly left the shop to Henry, and she didn't interfere with what had become the more 'interesting' side of the family business.

He worked on those artifacts in the basement levels after dark.

The jeweler's shop sat in between, and that suited Henry. He had always existed between cultures, at home in many, and at the same time, belonging to none. His Malaysian father had also been a jeweler, arriving in Poland on a cultural exchange where he had met a young blonde goldsmith.

The relationship only lasted a summer, and as his mother was a Catholic, Henry was born under the shadow of shame, kept hidden in his early years because he didn't look Polish. Some mixed race Malaysian-Europeans had features that combined the beauty of both cultures. But Henry knew he was not so blessed, bullied at school for the way he looked and his bastard outsider status.

His father eventually married the 'right kind of girl' and cut off his European-born son. Henry had never been to Malaysia, but then he had no wish to. For all his mother's guilt, she had only ever encouraged him in his art and since they visited the basilica almost every day, Henry grew up around the extravagance of the Catholic Church. He remained entranced by the gold and riches around him — but also by the portrayals of suffering.

His mother had inherited the house and the jeweler's business after the death of her father, and now Henry was the last in the family line of goldsmiths. All of them had been skilled artisans, but he intended that his legacy would last the longest.

He turned back to the sketch of the brooch. Something was missing. Henry stood and pulled down a book on Russian Orthodox icons from the surrounding shelves. His great-grandfather had started this library, and it was a precious resource for ideas. Religious art needed to resonate with a long-held tradition, but Henry still liked to bring something unique to each piece.

Shouts came from the street and then the raucous

laughter of tourists on their way to one of the local bars. Henry wondered how people could spend their time so frivolously, drinking precious minutes away. He didn't even like to sleep, a pattern of insomnia he had cultivated since childhood. Back then, he wandered the streets in the early hours of the morning, staying in the shadows, observing the homeless and unwanted, witnessing violent deeds. He crept back into bed before his mother rose for work, his body humming with energy, his mind alive with ideas.

One night, he found the fresh corpse of a cat near the steps of the basilica. It was so thin he could see almost every bone in its body, and the sleek lines reminded him of the shining white fragments within the reliquaries inside the church. Longing to make something so beautiful from the dead, he hid the corpse behind the bins out the back of the house and asked his mother for a space where he could work on his own projects.

"Will it be for the glory of God, Henry?"

He nodded at her words and basked in the smile of pride she bestowed upon him.

"Then take the basement level as your own. It needs cleaning up as it remains as your grandfather left it." She crossed herself. "May he rest in peace. I prefer to work upstairs in the natural light, so it can be yours. But you need to produce pieces for the shop and if they sell, I'll give you more freedom and the supplies you need."

Henry had reassured her of his dedication to the family business and that was the beginning of a new artistic direction.

The cat had been his first subject and over time, he experimented with different ways of removing fur and flesh. After he reduced a corpse down to bone, he experimented with techniques to age it in an attempt to recreate the distinctive patina of ancient relics.

He pulled up the flagstones in one section of the basement

to reveal the earth beneath and buried bones there, but it was an inefficient and slow process. On a taxidermy forum online, he discovered the use of strong tea, coffee, or even watered down shoe polish for a darker stain, but it didn't quite produce the desired effect. Henry even experimented with passing fragments through an animal, which could only be done with the tiniest pieces. He caged a mangy dog in the basement for the purpose, but something about its pitiful eyes made the process distasteful. Dogs did not worship body parts of their species, so they should not suffer for the faith of those who did.

Over time, Henry honed his craft, both in precious metals and in the processing of animal bones that lay within the reliquaries they sold in the shop, and increasingly online for a global market. His mother never questioned the provenance of the bones, only delighting in being able to retire off the profits of his work. He thought she must know what he did, but her silence implied acceptance, so he continued.

But Henry grew bored with his work, longing to create some truly extraordinary pieces and there were darker questions he wished to investigate. Would his aging methods work on human bones? How could he make his relics even more authentic?

Five years ago, a petite American woman with the unmistakable air of wealth walked into his jewelry shop and picked out one of his most elaborate golden brooches with a sliver of bone in the center.

"Do you take commissions?"

Her words marked the beginning of their lucrative relationship, but it wasn't so much about the money anymore. Dr. Kelley Montague-Breton was his main private client now and Henry truly loved the challenge of creating a perfect replica of the reliquaries she asked for.

He also enjoyed the preparation of the bones.

Kelley sent slivers sourced ethically from her biomedical

company, but she would never know the real provenance of the bone he included.

His art was not just in the fine metalwork and finished jeweled pieces; it was in the death of the martyr, whose fragments of bone or drops of blood lay within. The details had to be correct and Henry liked to think that the martyrs he created retained the power of those they replaced. Killing them in the same way was an important part of the process.

* * *

As Morgan looked around the basilica, she had to hand it to the Catholics. When it came to iconography and extravagant decoration in praise of God, they won hands down. Jewish synagogues were mostly plain and undecorated, with a focus on interior worship and the power of the written word. This place was almost the exact opposite.

The basilica was an overwhelming explosion of color. The walls were deep terracotta red and high above, the vaulted ceiling was Marian blue speckled with stars. Polished gold frames surrounded images of martyred saints reflecting light from flickering candles. Fresco and paint, carvings and tiles, and swirls of color in every shade of creation covered every inch. The scent of incense and candle smoke filled the air along with the sound of whispered prayers from the faithful who knelt at altars around the edges of the nave, each niche dedicated to a different saint.

Some places of worship felt empty and lifeless, but Morgan could sense the palpable faith here. Perhaps it was the warmth of color surrounding them, or the respite from the cold outside, but she would have loved more time to sit here in contemplation.

The painted vault of heaven on the ceiling above reminded her of the temple of Hatshepsut in Luxor, Egypt, which she and Jake once visited on a mission to find the Ark of the Covenant. A vault of stars on a midnight blue sky still remained there after more than three thousand years. The gods might have changed since then, but the nature of faith remained and humanity had always found the ineffable in the night sky above.

Morgan followed Jake down the nave, their footsteps echoing on the marble tiles. The grandeur of the basilica's decoration intensified with frescoes of angels and words of faith inscribed on the walls as they approached the main altar.

The fifteenth-century Veit Stoss altarpiece was a national treasure of Poland and one of the largest Gothic altarpieces in Europe. Stolen by the Nazis as part of plundered art and religious objects, it had been hidden in Nuremberg Castle, where it survived heavy bombardment during the Second World War and finally returned to the basilica in 1957. Six panels surrounded a central display, each with carved figures made from linden wood depicting scenes from the life of Mary, mother of Christ. The central panel showed the Dormition in the presence of the Apostles, when the Theotokos, Mother of God, fell asleep before being taken up to Heaven.

Morgan pointed to the top of the altarpiece, where more statues perched in glory. "That's the Coronation of Mary. She's flanked by Saint Adalbert of Prague and Saint Stanislaus. We need to find his relic."

They walked in opposite directions back down the edges of the basilica, examining each of the niches. Morgan found lots of interesting saints, but no Stanislaus on her side. Turning at the end, she noticed Jake had stopped halfway down to examine one altar in more detail. She walked back to join him.

A wooden rail separated the niche from the main nave so they couldn't get too close, but underneath the statue of the saint, Morgan could make out a gold filigree box with a tiny glass window. A sliver of bone lay inside, a handwritten label with the name of the saint attached with crimson thread.

The King of Poland had martyred the medieval Bishop Stanislaus when his knights refused to cut down the man of God. After his death, they scattered his body parts to be devoured by wild beasts, but legend says that they were miraculously reintegrated.

Jake bent forward as far as he could, squinting at the tiny reliquary for a moment, then he shrugged. "These holy bones all look the same to me."

Morgan couldn't help but smile because she knew exactly what he meant. But then, they were not believers and would never understand how the bones of a saint could have such deep meaning.

Her phone buzzed with a message. "It's Martin. He cross-matched the work of jewelers who specialize in religious objects with the batch of gold. One artisan has a shop just a few streets away."

CHAPTER 6

Morgan peered into the window of the Palarae jeweler's shop. While other stores in the area were crammed with lurid goods designed to tempt the tourist masses, this display was artfully arranged with just a few beautiful pieces. Clearly, an artisan jeweler for the discerning religious collector with money to spend for the glory of God.

Jake pushed the door open, and a bell rang inside. Morgan followed him in. The shop had high ceilings and large windows that allowed the late afternoon sunlight to illuminate the treasures within. One wall had religious icons of different sizes, most of the Virgin Mary but some of tortured saints and the crucified Christ.

A man walked out from the back room wearing a three-piece suit of midnight blue, tailored to emphasize his long limbs, and expensive enough to impress potential clients. He was mixed race with Asian heritage, thick dark hair combed neatly into a side parting. While he would easily blend into a more international city, his difference stood out in this more homogenous culture, and Morgan wondered how that might have shaped his life.

"Dzień dobry," he welcomed them in Polish with a smile that didn't quite reach his eyes. He exuded an air of confident expectation rather than the deference of a sales clerk. Perhaps this was the jeweler himself.

"Morning," Jake said.

"Ah, you're British?"

Jake grinned. "Something like that."

Morgan understood his smile. They were both untethered somehow, never quite feeling at home. Jake was South African, she was raised in Israel and both of them had British mothers, but their ties to their adopted country were complicated at the best of times.

"Can I help you with anything in particular?" The man pulled a tray out from beneath the counter full of intricate gold rings with religious symbols, some set with precious stones. They glinted in the sunlight that filtered through the windows, reflecting a rainbow of colors onto the Catholic icons around them.

The jeweler clearly knew his potential clientele, as Morgan couldn't help but bend to look more closely, even though she rarely wore jewelry. She kept one of her mother's rings in the memory trunk in her attic back in Oxford, but given the active nature of their ARKANE missions, she preferred to remain free of anything that might be lost or used against her.

One sapphire ring was a shade of blue that reminded her of the Mediterranean Sea off the coast of Israel. She had swum there with her father under sunny skies back in the days before she knew true darkness.

Morgan reached out a fingertip and touched the ring. It was cool, and she imagined the weight of it on her hand.

"Try it on," the jeweler said, his tone soft and persuasive.

His words jolted Morgan from her reverie, and she shook her head. "Thank you, but we're not here to shop."

She pulled out her phone and swiped to the picture of the Becket reliquary, then held it out to the jeweler. "We're looking for someone who could have made this."

The jeweler bent to look closely at the image. "It's fine work, but if I'm not mistaken, that is a medieval reliquary, not a modern piece."

"Chemical analysis of the gold traced a batch to this area," Jake explained. "Perhaps you know of an artisan skilled enough to make such a thing?"

The jeweler shook his head. "I'm sorry, but none of the artisans I know would create a fake." He put his hands together over his heart. "We are people of faith. Such a thing would not be acceptable to God."

Morgan found his choice of words unusual, but it was the look in his eyes that made her doubt him. He recognized the reliquary; she was sure of it.

Jake pulled out a card with a contact phone number and laid it on the display case.

"If you think of anyone, please let us know."

The jeweler nodded. "Of course. Are you staying in the city long?"

"It depends on what we find," Jake said.

As they walked out of the shop into the street beyond, Morgan turned back to look through the window. The jeweler stood staring down at the card as if he couldn't quite decide what to do with it. There was something about him that made the hairs on the back of her neck bristle, something in his examining gaze that suggested he knew more than he would say.

* * *

Henry Palarae waited until they were out of sight before turning the sign on the door to 'Closed.' The woman had looked back for a moment, but they seemed to believe him for now and that gave him enough time to figure out what to do. His heart still pounded from the moment he had seen the picture of the reliquary. It seemed impossible that they had traced him back here, but no matter, it would be dealt with soon enough.

He walked back to the little office behind the storefront, and played the security footage from the encounter on his laptop. He zoomed into the face of the man, frozen in an expression of curiosity as he looked around the shop. Henry was intrigued by the corkscrew scar above the man's left eyebrow and the way he carried himself, like a big cat with barely restrained power in his muscles. He was clearly ex-military, and in ancient times, he could have fought and won in the arenas of the Roman Empire, one of Henry's favorite times of history. They truly understood how to martyr the faithful back then. This man's bones would be strong and stand up well to the aging process, and a glimmer of an idea began to form as to what he might become.

Henry smiled as he emailed the footage to Zale Radan at Anchorite with a few sparse words that he knew the security chief would appreciate: *Deal with the woman. Bring the man to me. Usual terms.*

The task complete, Henry exhaled slowly. The end of a day up here in the shop meant he could descend to where he truly felt at home. He locked the front door and pulled down the metal security shutters, turned off the lights, and opened the thick wooden door to the basement.

He had to bend a little as he stepped through the small doorway, designed for generations much shorter than his tall frame. It was awkward to fold himself into the medieval building, but that only added to Henry's sense that he had expanded into the world far more than those before him.

The room below was dim, lit only by an emerald green glow from a single decorative lamp on an oversized table. There was a modern powerful craft lamp next to it used for delicate work, but Henry liked to retain a historical atmosphere when he sat down to create. There was one window high up that opened onto a side street, but he only opened it after the sound of the city sank to a murmur.

The tools of the jeweler's trade lay on the table — ring

cutters, pin setters, shapers, and files of different grades. Some were old, handed down through generations of artisans, each with a lineage of craft that Henry tried to channel in his art. Others were new and his aim was to imbibe them with his own history, so they might be handed on in turn. A pile of sketchbooks sat on one side of the table, the uppermost open to a sketch of a thirteenth-century golden reliquary in the shape of a forearm, dotted with jewels, with a space for the long bone of a saint.

There were more sketchbooks in tall fitted shelving amongst tomes on religious art and the history of precious metals. One wall was constructed of wooden drawers in varying sizes, each with a copper plate etched with symbols that would confuse all but the expert jeweler.

The workshop smelled of old books and metal shavings with a hint of warm leather from the armchair in one corner next to which stood a drinks cabinet. Henry poured himself a generous measure of aged *slivovitz* and sat down in the chair, pulling another sketchbook onto his lap. He found that the designs he created down here truly reflected his inner self. Perhaps the deeper he descended physically, the more he could access his creative subconscious.

Henry smiled as he sketched the martyrdom of Saint Sebastian. Hands bound, taut muscles pierced by arrows — and a corkscrew scar marking a handsome face transfigured with agony.

CHAPTER 7

Northumberland, England

Zale Radan finished the last set of one-armed push-ups just as his phone buzzed. He jumped to his feet and checked the message, a smile dawning as he read the words from the jeweler, Palarae. Zale's team had taken care of the Becket relic without him, but this was exactly what he needed to get away. He glanced over at the security monitors, checking each screen with a practiced gaze.

Everything was calm and quiet. Nothing moved in the compound.

Nothing except the shadows around the citadel that he could only see out of the corner of his eye, that never appeared on recorded footage, that he tried to pretend were just his imagination.

The freezing rain should have obscured them today, but shifting winds still caught handfuls of raindrops and whipped them into shapes of hunched beasts with savage claws and skeletal figures with hooded faces. He didn't want to go out there, but the imminent end of his security shift meant he needed to patrol. Technically, Zale was the compound commander and could roster himself off, but his men had to walk the gauntlet of shadow, and he took pride in doing the same work.

The sound of a helicopter came from outside, the chop chop of blades increasing in volume as it flew up the pass, the sound funneled by steep cliffs.

Zale rolled up the sleeves of his Anchorite Security uniform, the better to display the white slashes on his muscular forearms, scars from the Balkan War where he had learned his trade. He enjoyed security work — at least when it involved some action — and he looked the part. Zale's eyes bulged a little from their sockets because of a head injury sustained at the same time as the scars, and his nose had been broken too many times for it to ever look normal. Physical pain was temporary and Zale had proved he could take almost any amount of it. He wore his injuries with pride and had no fear of sustaining more.

But up here in the wilds of Northumberland, he had found something to fear.

The sound of the helicopter grew louder as it crested the ridge and hovered before coming to rest on the helipad on the cliff side of the compound. Zale stared down from the window, watching as the blades spun slowly to a halt.

Dr. Kelley Montague-Breton emerged from the side, her slight figure bent low against the rain as she hurried toward the main house. One of Zale's men rushed out to pick up her bags from the helicopter: a portable medical refrigeration unit marked with blood product stickers and a small personal case. She clearly wasn't staying long. But then she never stayed more than a night or two and only came when summoned. The estate was in Kelley's name, but she never brought her sons here. At least not according to the visitor records and they went back generations, handwritten in thick books bound with terracotta leather.

Zale flexed his biceps a few more times until the muscles strained against his uniform, then he left the security room.

He descended the staircase, his footsteps muffled by the thick green carpet woven with images of the wild woods of the North. Kelley stood in the hallway, shaking rain from her coat. She wore tight jeans over her slight figure and a black leather jacket that only highlighted her freckled skin and strawberry blonde curls. It was a shame she came so infrequently because there was precious little else to look at when he was confined to the estate for so long.

She looked up as Zale approached, her gaze flickering over his muscular frame. Her face was pinched and her perfectly applied makeup couldn't hide the dark shadows under her eyes or the tension in her jaw. But this was how she always looked when she arrived, and Zale only wished he could help her bear the strain of the trials ahead.

"How are things?"

"Same as usual. Nothing to report."

Kelley nodded. "I'm only here long enough to give him this." She pointed at the refrigeration unit.

"Of course. Is there anything else you need?"

The implication was clear in his words and Kelley half-smiled. "Do you have the Becket relic?"

Zale nodded. "It's in the safe."

"I'll take it in with me. Bring it to the library in twenty minutes. I just need to freshen up."

She walked away down the corridor toward her private quarters, and Zale watched her go. Damn, he wished he could tap that. Although truth be told, he really wanted to keep her close and protect her — from the man who dwelt within the citadel.

Zale had never seen the Black Anchorite, but his presence pervaded the estate. A blind servant who spoke little English tended to his needs. What little they were. She took over meager supplies of food, not nearly enough for two people to subsist on, and also carried in the books that sustained the Black Anchorite and were his only real expense.

Strange for a man who controlled such a vast fortune.

Zale had spent some time delving into his employer. Anchorite Holdings held a vast amount of land across Europe, from swathes of the coast in Israel to streets of shops in the medieval heart of Prague, and vineyards in the South of France. It was bound up with myriad companies, including a majority stake in Breton Biochemical amongst others.

Anchorite Security, one of its subsidiaries, had stations all over Europe, the Middle East and the USA. An elite security firm with contracts at the highest level of government, it provided backup to the military and corporations alike, but few in the wider organization knew of its elusive founder, and even fewer had visited the estate in the wilds of Northumberland. Zale had proven himself to be both effective and discreet in the field, and this job was his reward — although it was a mixed blessing.

The estate was a strange place with little active security work. It was mostly surveillance to ensure the compound remained protected at all times. The job was boring, but it was also one of the highest paid within Anchorite — and Zale really loved money.

He hoarded it and invested it and used different apps on his phone to model his growing portfolio. Every day he worked added more cash to his account, and more was always the goal. The money kept him here even on the days when he wanted to flee this place and leave its twisted shadows to over-run the estate. Zale had a number in mind and his bank account ticked relentlessly toward it, faster when he took the extra jobs from Palarae the jeweler. They were off-book, but usually worked within the missions for relic recovery. Not too much longer and he could leave this place. He only wished he could help Kelley escape her entanglement, but her roots wound deep into this land, and the Black Anchorite's hold, whatever it might be, could not be easily broken.

Zale returned to the security suite and took the Becket reliquary from the safe. It was much smaller than some of the others they'd stolen on demand, but clearly, this fragment of bone was valuable.

He carried it to the library and paced up and down in front of the empty fireplace. The library was a repository for the books sent back out of the citadel, and every few years, the oldest crumbling tomes were carried down into the cavernous cellars to make room for more. Sturdy walnut-wood shelves stretched up to the ceiling, every space filled with accumulated pages of knowledge on every subject. Some spines were unreadable, their titles worn away by time, and many were in different languages, some marked with curious symbols. Zale wondered how many lifetimes it would take to read them all.

The room smelled of mould, damp, and rotting leather. A roaring fire and a fleet of dehumidifiers would fix it in a few weeks, but Kelley had shaken her head at his suggestion last time she was here. "Let it die," she said. Zale wondered if she was really talking about the library.

Footsteps came from the hallway and Kelley walked in, now wearing dark green hospital scrubs, her face clean of makeup, her curls tied back. Her expression was set with determination, but she clutched her hands together, her knuckles white with restrained tension. Zale wished he could go with her into the citadel, but she refused all help. It was her burden alone and besides, there were rumors that others who had entered never emerged back into the light.

Kelley joined Zale by the fireplace, standing close as if to draw from his heat and strength. He wished he could pull her into his arms, but although she flirted with him sometimes, she had never made it clear she would accept his advances. He would be ready when she did.

As Zale pulled the Becket reliquary from his pocket and handed it to her, their fingers touched briefly. The golden artifact looked much bigger in her tiny hand, but Zale knew that delicacy only camouflaged her medical skill. Kelley could heal, but she could also disassemble a human body far more effectively than he ever could. A scalpel blade in her hand was more deadly than his fists and he respected her for that.

She looked up at him, her blue eyes sharp and focused. "I'll take it in. Hopefully, it's enough to keep his mind off… the procedure."

"You've never told me what you do in there."

Kelley exhaled slowly and shook her head. "It's better that you don't know. I'll see you after."

She walked out of the library, her pace quickening as if she wanted to get the task over and done with. Zale went back up to the security suite and watched from the window as Kelley crossed the courtyard and stood in front of the citadel, the medical unit in her hand.

The massive wooden door studded with iron rivets opened before her and as she stepped inside, it seemed as if the inner darkness swallowed her whole.

The citadel was the oldest building at the heart of the estate, built from stones torn from a pagan temple. A great battle had been fought on this escarpment in ancient times, and legend said that the bones and blood of the fallen were plowed into the land as an offering to a malevolent spirit that demanded sacrifice.

Whatever the truth of its construction, Zale was careful not to walk too close and advised his men to stay several meters back from the citadel's stone walls when on patrol. Despite this warning, the smell of the place still clung to their clothes. Smoke from the pyres of burned heretics and rotten vegetation filled with the corpses of children sacrificed to the old gods.

The shadows didn't quite match its stone contours and seemed to creep closer when clouds hid the sun. Too long on patrol gave rise to a sense of despair and some of Zale's men told of nightmares filled with clawed hands rising from the grave. He wouldn't admit it out loud, but he had seen such things in his sleep, too.

He paced up and down as he waited for Kelley to re-emerge, his gaze fixed on the huge wooden door, fists clenched in frustration at not being able to help her.

*   *   *

Zale was still watching when Kelley stumbled out of the citadel door several hours later. She leaned against the massive stone wall, her hand braced for support as she sucked in deep breaths of fresh air. Her skin was even paler than before and she was shaking so much she could barely stand. She no longer carried the medical box and dark clots of blood spotted her scrubs. Looking up at the sky, she let the rain soak her through, as if it could wash away her burden along with the bloodstains. Zale wanted to run down and help her, but he knew she didn't want anyone to see her, weak and debilitated by whatever she faced in there.

A few minutes later, Kelley walked slowly to the side door that led to her private rooms. She slumped with exhaustion, every footstep hard won. Zale switched his surveillance to the camera outside her room, the closest he dared to place such a device.

Half an hour later, Kelley emerged, her skin scrubbed pink as if she had tried to scrape the top layer away, her hair freshly washed and tied back from her face. She might have looked younger than her years, but her eyes were haunted and stress lines etched her perfect skin.

Zale hurried down to meet her once more in the library. She paced up and down, her energy renewed now she was away from the shadowed citadel, her task accomplished.

"How was it?" he asked.

She waved a hand as if to brush away his concern. "It's done, at least for the time being. But he has another task for you."

Zale nodded. "Of course. What does he need?"

"You have to go to Cologne in Germany. He wants the relics of the Magi." She hesitated a moment before continuing. "Particularly the long bones."

Zale frowned as he considered why the Black Anchorite would need such a thing. "I'll do some research and start preparations."

Kelley put her hand on his arm. "I'll go back to London tonight. Call me once you have the relics, as I need to return for the delivery. Perhaps then we might have a drink… or something."

She smiled up at him and Zale could only hope that was a promise in her eyes. As he walked back to his office to plan the trip to Cologne, he considered the message from Palarae the jeweler. Perhaps there was a way to achieve two goals with one trip.

CHAPTER 8

Cologne, Germany

SOME CATHEDRALS SOARED INTO the sky, capturing the glory of God and reflecting it back to heaven. Kölner Dom, the Cathedral Church of St Peter in Cologne, was not one of those places. At least it wasn't in the gloom of an approaching rainstorm under heavy clouds that bruised the winter sky.

Morgan and Jake stood in Domplatte surrounded by busy commuters heading home. Grey offices around the edge of the square echoed the shades of smoke and steel that peppered the concrete blocks under their feet. The cathedral was one of the tallest churches in the world and it loomed over them against the backdrop of the city, imposing its will like the vengeful God of the Old Testament. Acid rain had blackened its sandstone facade, further emphasizing the Gothic arches and flying buttresses that swept up toward its twin spires. Some of the more recent carvings and statues around the entrance stood out with their lighter color, and Morgan thought the cathedral must once have been a marvel to behold. It was still one of the most visited pilgrimage sites in Northern Europe, but its dark shadow conjured a sense of divine judgment.

Perhaps the real treasure lay inside.

The jeweler Henry Palarae had left a message last night on the number from Jake's card suggesting that one of the ecclesiastical art restorers at Cologne Cathedral had links with a circle of art thieves. The cathedral had its own workshop and the full-time artisans were kept busy by the march of entropy, but it was also a viable lead. Morgan still had her doubts about Palarae, but it was only a few hours' flight from Kraków and they had exhausted their options in Poland, at least for now.

While the site had been a place of worship since the Roman era, this Gothic cathedral was constructed in medieval times as a fitting location for the relics of the Magi, the Three Kings who attended the birth of Christ, according to Scripture. Once housed in Constantinople, the relics were moved to Milan in the fourth century, but a more illustrious shrine was needed for such precious relics and they were transported here in 1164.

Some believed that the relics protected the cathedral during the Allied bombing in the Second World War. The city was flattened, and the cathedral hit fourteen times, but it remained standing with its twin spires intact. Morgan wondered if it was perhaps more of a testament to their use as a navigational landmark than spiritual protection, but she kept an open mind about these things.

A roll of thunder sounded across the city and the smatter of rain intensified. People in the square hurried for shelter, and Morgan and Jake walked quickly up the steps into the cathedral.

As she stepped inside, Morgan couldn't help but smile. For all its disappointing exterior darkness, the cathedral was a glorious Gothic marvel within. Five aisles of slender pillars with statues of the saints mounted upon them led up to a soaring vault. With no acid rain to darken the stone, the architectural beauty swept her gaze upward. High windows with intricate stained glass arched above and even though rain hammered down outside, light filled the cathedral. The sense of insignificance in the face of such beauty never failed to remind Morgan of how swiftly an individual life passed by. Some of these stones had stood for a thousand years, a witness to the generations who came to seek solace and guidance in the church.

She looked over at Jake. "Let's check out the shrine behind the high altar before we track down the artisan workshop."

As they walked down the nave over the crossing, Morgan noticed a tour group near the end of the north transept by a statue of a modern saint leaning on a crucifix staff. A tour guide explained it had a relic inside, a piece of cloth with a drop of blood from Pope John Paul II. Her voice was muted, but the perfect acoustics of the space carried her German-accented English. Morgan wished they had more time to explore as every meter of the cathedral contained fascinating ecclesiastical history that she was sure held more mysteries. But time ticked toward the moment when the current Pope would kneel in prayer in Canterbury and they were running out of time.

Morgan and Jake walked past ornate choir stalls with over one hundred carved oak seats. Intricate mosaics in rich colors covered the floor, depicting scenes from the Bible and spiritual figures throughout the ages. Above them, larger-than-life figures of the Twelve Apostles with Jesus and Mary looked down with beneficent eyes while angels danced around them in celebration. Each Apostle was painted in intricate detail with muted colors inlaid with gold and carried their symbol of faith or martyrdom: Peter held the keys to heaven, Matthew clutched an axe, while Simon gripped the saw that ripped his body apart.

Individual worshippers knelt in prayer or sat in contemplation on wooden pews, the space between them providing privacy. Each looked tiny against the backdrop of the church and Morgan could only imagine the grandeur of the nave filled with voices praising God during a full service. It would be glorious indeed.

They walked around the ambulatory, past the Altar of the Crucifixion to the Shrine of the Magi.

"That's some serious bling," Jake whispered.

The golden shrine shone so brightly under the spotlights that it was hard to make out the carvings. Shaped like a basilica with a triple sarcophagus design, each side was decorated with filigree, enamel and precious jewels. Figures from the Bible were portrayed in relief: the prophets, apostles and evangelists alongside scenes from the Adoration of the Magi, the life of Jesus, and Christ enthroned at the Last Judgment. Inside lay bones and shreds of cloth, documented when the shrine had been opened in 1864, and whose provenance was sustained by the faith of believers.

As Morgan bent to look closer, a sudden commotion came from the entrance to the cathedral and the sounds of shouting drew their attention away from the shrine.

Automatic gunfire.

Screams from worshippers at prayer.

Morgan ducked down, her heart hammering as Jake crouched beside her. They were unarmed with no backup — and she had a feeling this was no coincidence.

She crawled to the side of the shrine and peered down the aisle.

Six men in black uniforms with no insignia stormed down the nave, balaclavas hiding their faces. One led from the front while the others fanned out around the cathedral. Two men remained by the main door, weapons raised as they urged people to stay down.

One of the congregation stood up and shouted at the men, clearly defending his faith and his place of worship. A spray of gunfire and the man collapsed to the floor, his blood running across the colorful mosaics.

One more martyr to the cause.

A hail of lead thudded into the pews of the ancient church, leaving scars of violence in the wood as they splintered under the force. One bullet hit an icon of the crucified Christ, cracking the paint that had provided centuries of protection. Slivers of crimson dropped to the marble beneath, as if the Savior gave his body once again for the forgiveness of this latest sin.

Another round slammed through one of the stained glass windows, raining shards of glass down on the faithful below. Wind whipped through the hole, blowing rain into the cathedral, and the acrid stench of metal and smoke filled the air of the sanctuary.

The invaders hurried toward the Shrine of the Magi, no doubt aware that the German police would be on their way. The leader of the group was a bull of a man with thick muscular arms that stretched the seams of his uniform and a military-style pack on his back.

"They're coming this way," Morgan whispered. "Let's move."

Jake pointed to the shrines on either side. "You go that way, I'll hide over there so we can see what's going on."

He darted over to the Chapel of John, using the thick stone walls to shield him from view. Morgan ran across to the Chapel of St Agnes and ducked down behind the altar rail. She could see the choir area clearly through the metal filigree and watched the men approach the shrine with confident strides.

The leader swung off his pack and pulled out a heavy crowbar as the other men ranged around him with guns at the ready.

He smashed the glass with one swing.

A shrill alarm sounded, but he ignored it, using the crowbar to hack away the remaining glass. He inserted the end into a seam in the shrine and used his weight to split it open.

The crack of metal and splintering of wood pierced the air and beneath the shouts in the nave, Morgan sensed the heartbreak of the faithful who cowered under the weapons of the invaders. This was more than a theft, it was a violation of holy ground.

The leader pulled a padded wooden box from his pack and beckoned to two of the men. They dragged a pew over for him to stand on so he could lean over the open shrine and reach in. The sarcophagus was too heavy to steal, but it looked like they weren't here for gold and jewels, only for the spiritual treasure inside.

Morgan glimpsed the bones as the leader carefully lifted them out of the sarcophagus and gently placed them in the padded box. It was impossible to know whose bones they really were, but whoever wanted them clearly believed in their power.

It had to be the same people who stole the Becket reliquary.

The man jumped down from the pew and closed the box, securely locking it before turning around to look at the chapels behind the shrine.

Morgan ducked back behind the altar rail, hoping that Jake was also out of sight. They were unarmed and pinned down with no way to escape.

"I know you're here. Jake Timber and Morgan Sierra. Agents of ARKANE."

The man's deep voice was audible despite the shrill beeps of the alarm. He had an Eastern European accent, perhaps from the Balkan region, but it was hard to tell with the balaclava and the noise in the cathedral.

"I don't have time for a fight, so I'll be quick. Jake Timber comes with us now and I spare a child's life. But not just any child."

He pulled out his phone and tapped the screen, holding it out toward the half moon of the surrounding chapels as it played the slightly distorted sound of children giggling. Morgan frowned in confusion. Then she heard Gemma's voice — her niece laughing as she played with a friend. They must have someone at the primary school back in Oxford.

Morgan covered her mouth to hold back a scream. She was too far away to help Gemma, and there was no way anyone else could reach her niece in time. Her family had almost died during the hunt for the Pentecost stones, and Morgan had vowed to keep them safe.

Whatever the cost.

CHAPTER 9

As Jake heard Gemma's laughter, he knew Morgan's heart would be breaking. Her niece was precious, and keeping Gemma safe and away from the danger of their missions was paramount. He didn't have any family left, at least not blood relatives. His father, mother and two sisters were butchered by a drug-fueled gang in South Africa many years ago and although he still thought of his family, the detail of their faces had faded along with the photograph he kept in his wallet. Morgan would never ask him for this sacrifice, but he would make sure that Gemma returned safely home tonight.

"I'm coming out," Jake called from behind the wall of the chapel.

He clenched his fists in anticipation of the inevitable violence ahead, but part of him relished the opportunity to face those behind the theft of the relics. The jeweler had been their only lead, but they really wanted the people he worked for. If Jake went with these men, he had no doubt that Morgan would be close behind.

He trusted his ARKANE partner — more than that; they shared a bond that went beyond work. They both knew it, but their feelings remained unspoken for the sake of the job and, perhaps, to prevent the pain of inevitable loss.

ARKANE agents didn't have a long life expectancy, and they had both lost people they loved.

Jake raised his hands to shoulder height, palms forward, and stepped out into the ambulatory.

The leader of the relic thieves turned, his expression masked by the balaclava, but his posture shifted to one of readiness. The men beside him pointed their weapons at Jake, although he was more than outnumbered. It would be suicide to try and disarm them, even with Morgan's help.

Jake walked slowly to the front of the shrine, hands still raised in surrender. "You'll leave the girl alone?"

The leader nodded and spoke a few words in what could have been Albanian, or possibly Bulgarian, before putting the phone back in his jacket. "It is done. Now we go."

He gestured to the other men. They surrounded Jake and marched him double time down the nave. As the sound of police sirens grew louder outside, the leader followed at a jog, the padded box with the bones of the Magi safely in his pack.

* * *

Morgan stepped out from the chapel and watched them head toward the main door. She understood her partner and could almost imagine Jake's thoughts as the men marched him away. He knew she would follow. Jake had put himself at the mercy of violent men for the sake of her family, and she would not stop until he was safe again.

A sudden break in the clouds and a beam of sunlight lanced in through the stained glass windows high above, catching the group of men at the door. For a moment, it looked as if Jake walked through a halo into the world beyond.

Morgan's breath caught as a sense of foreboding rose within her. They had always found each other before, but what if their luck ran out this time?

A cry escaped her lips. "Jake, no!"

He turned back to face her with a calm smile, even as the men with guns at the ready surrounded him. Morgan couldn't do a thing as one man put a hood over Jake's head and pulled him roughly out the door, followed closely by the leader holding the relic box.

The last soldier fired his automatic weapon into the nave, a spray of bullets thudding into the pews.

Morgan ducked behind the chapel wall, her back against the stone, her mind reeling as she considered her next step.

A door slammed. Gunfire came from outside, then the screech of vehicles pulling away.

The bones of the Magi were gone — and so was Jake.

*   *   *

As the police entered the cathedral to process the incident, Morgan slipped away through the sacristy and chapter house to the public square beyond. She couldn't be caught up in the red tape of a criminal investigation when every minute counted in tracking Jake.

The rain intensified as Morgan walked away into the maze of city streets. She pulled out her phone as soon as she was out of sight of the plaza, called Martin, and quickly explained the situation.

"You need to get on the German CCTV cameras and track those men out of here."

Morgan heard the tapping of his fingers even before she finished speaking. She held the phone like a lifeline as she waited, every second stretching out for too long. She was desperate to move, to jump in a taxi and follow, but there was no point acting too soon.

"The men left in two cars and headed in different directions," Martin said. "Jake's in one, the guy with the box is in the other."

"Follow Jake." Morgan's response was immediate. The dead bones could wait.

"The car headed south west… it's pulling into Hiroshima-Nagasaki Park just minutes from you… there's a helicopter. It's touching down in the park."

Morgan bit her lip as a heaviness descended upon her. There was no way she could prevent them from taking Jake now. Martin could track the helicopter, but they would be well ahead of her and could land pretty much anywhere in Europe. She didn't know why they wanted him, but it certainly wasn't for tea and cake.

"Follow the helicopter. What about the other car, the one with the bones?" And the leader of the group, who Morgan would dearly like to spend some quality time with.

More tapping.

"The helicopter carrying Jake is in the air. I've tagged it so we'll know when it lands. The other car went northeast… Looks like they're heading for a private airport, Flugplatz Leverkusen. I'll monitor departing flights. We'll find him, Morgan. By the time you get to the airport, I'll have more of an idea which direction to go and I'll have transport waiting."

Morgan leaned back against the stone wall and turned her face up to the rain. The cold numbed her skin and trickled down into her jacket. She thought of Jake, hooded and bound, perhaps already beaten.

"Hold on," she whispered. "I'm coming for you."

* * *

Jake slowly emerged from a fog of whatever drug they'd injected him with, his head thumping, his limbs leaden. He lay on his back on a cold floor, hands and feet bound, hood still over his head. He tried to roll, but his feet were anchored to something, and as he drew his knees up a little, he heard a metal clank of chain.

He breathed in, sucking the hood against his mouth for a moment. It tasted of sweat and still held the stink of helicopter fuel. But it was loose enough, so they clearly wanted him alive. He also hadn't been beaten, which was a nice surprise. But what was the fun of torturing an unconscious subject? He rather thought they were saving it for when he was awake.

Which meant the time was ticking closer.

He could only hope that Morgan made it before whoever it was did some serious damage.

Jake tuned in his other senses. It was quiet, as if the world was on mute. Either he was a long way from civilization or he was deep underground. The air was stagnant. There was no window, no crack in the stone for a fresh breeze to sweep the miasma away. It smelled of earth and wet stone and underneath, something metallic. Not just the metal restraints, but a hint of old blood and the marrow from broken bones.

The sound of footsteps came from above and drew closer down stone steps.

The door creaked a little and something metal scraped on the flagstones. Jake's heart raced as he prepared to meet his captor, clenching his fingers and toes rhythmically to get his blood moving. If he had any chance to move, he would take it.

The click of a switch.

Light flooded the hood, and Jake screwed his eyes shut against the sudden glare. He sensed someone moving closer, and he readied himself to act, rehearsing a jack-knife and a head-butt in his mind that would leave his captor reeling.

A metal clank and the tension on his handcuffs changed. Whoever it was had attached something to his restraints.

The sound of hydraulics and his hands began to rise. The machine pulled him to a sitting position and then continued upward. With his feet still fastened to some kind of chain on the ground, Jake couldn't move.

He didn't fight it, saving his energy for when he might have a glimmer of hope of escaping. As his arms were tugged above his head, Jake went with the movement until he stood, arms attached above him, feet shackled below.

The noise of the hydraulic pump stopped and in the quiet, Jake could hear the breathing of the person in the room with him. He was determined not to speak first, and he would stall as much as he could. Every second of delay gave Morgan more time to find him. He knew she would come. The only question was whether he would still be alive by the time she made it.

The hydraulics pulsed again and pulled his arms even higher until he arched back, his toes just off the floor, suspended between his restraints. Any hope of head-butting his captor was gone. This was a well-practiced routine, and Jake wondered how many people had died here before him.

He breathed in and then exhaled, slowly relaxing his muscles, calming his racing heart.

The hood was snatched off his head in one movement, and Jake blinked in the bright glare. A man stood in front of him, silhouetted against two bright floodlights, the kind that photographers used to illuminate a subject.

As Jake's eyes adjusted, he saw it was the jeweler, Henry Palarae. Clearly, there was a darker side to the artisan's creativity.

He could see his surroundings more clearly now: a stone basement with thick walls and no windows. There were many such places in the heart of medieval cities, tunnels deep below the earth, perfect for storage or hiding places — or violent acts committed away from prying eyes.

Palarae remained silent as he assessed Jake's body, tilting his head to one side as he circled his victim, staying well back. The jeweler was clearly no fool. Without these restraints, Jake knew he would be out of here in no time. Whatever drugs they'd given him had worn off and, in fact, his senses seemed heightened.

The jeweler walked behind one light and emerged holding a large pair of fabric shears, the silver blades flashing as he snipped at the air.

He nudged the hydraulics once more to make sure his victim could not move, then stepped close. He pulled Jake's shirt out of his jeans and used the shears to cut the material away, exposing his muscled chest, and then chopped the sleeves until the fabric fell to the stone beneath. Jake shivered as the cold metal blades brushed his chest and the underside of his arm.

Once Palarae had removed the shirt, the jeweler reached out one hand and traced the musculature of Jake's pectoral muscles. A flicker of a smile twitched at the corner of his mouth, but there was nothing sexual in the man's touch. It was more like an anatomist's appreciation for a physical specimen.

Palarae continued cutting until Jake stood only in a pair of boxer shorts, then the jeweler stood back, shears in hand as he examined his subject. After a moment, he nodded to himself and nudged the hydraulics until Jake's feet touched the ground. His arms continued to descend until he sagged a little against the restraints. It would easily take his weight if he collapsed under whatever tortures came next.

The jeweler emerged once more from behind the light and Jake's breath caught as he saw the weapon that Palarae held in his hands.

CHAPTER 10

Kraków, Poland

MORGAN WAS OUT OF the private plane before the engines even stopped spinning. She ran down the steps to the waiting car and jumped in the back. The driver revved the engines and headed off toward Stare Miasto, the medieval heart of the Old Town.

Martin Klein had traced the helicopter here, but he hadn't been able to track any cars or trucks leaving the airport after it arrived. Despite the lack of intel, there was only one person who Morgan suspected of holding Jake and if Henry Palarae didn't have her ARKANE partner, then he would tell her everything he knew. The jeweler could no longer hide behind his religious icons, and Morgan was in no mood for patience.

While she went after Jake, Martin concentrated on the primary mission. He had lost track of the helicopter containing the bones of the Magi and the leader of the relic thieves somewhere over western Germany. They used known gaps in surveillance areas and remote private airstrips to change vehicles several times, but Martin would use his vast databases and intelligence network to swiftly narrow down the possibilities. The Becket reliquary was clearly one of many, and Morgan was confident they'd be back on the primary mission soon enough. Right now, Jake was her only priority.

The car screeched to a halt at the edge of the pedestrianized area near the basilica. Morgan jumped out and ran to the jeweler's shop, bursting through the door as the bell rang over her head.

An old woman sat on a low stool at the back of the display cases, her body hunched over, her frame withered, her skin wrinkled. She wore a loose black smock and leaned on a thick wooden cane. The woman had the look of one who waited in death's approaching shadow, but her eyes were surprisingly alert.

"Dobry wieczór, can I help you?"

As much as Morgan wanted to rush past and ransack the place for Jake, he might not even be here. She needed to find the jeweler first.

"I'm looking for Henry Palarae."

The old woman sighed and slowly stood up from her stool, leaning on the cane as she struggled to her feet. Her hands shook with some kind of palsy, but her pale blue eyes were hard as sapphires with no hint of the weakness in her body.

Morgan had seen such a look in the eyes of those who survived war and adversity, sometimes through violence of their own. She remembered her father's friends, the tattooed remnant in the kibbutzim of Israel, who would gather in the dusk to remember the dead. Morgan learned never to startle them with her presence after one gnarled old man grabbed her by the throat, his eyes blazing with barely restrained fury. When people are broken and left for dead, some rise up with more strength than before.

"What do you want with my son?"

"Do you know where he is?"

The old woman gripped the handle of her cane and

shuffled out from behind the counter, then pointed out the door with one wrinkled hand.

"He's at prayer in the cathedral."

As Morgan's gaze automatically followed the old woman's outstretched hand, she glimpsed an almost imperceptible stiffening beneath the black smock in her peripheral vision.

A classic misdirection and she'd fallen for it.

The old woman flicked her cane, lashing it out with a practiced movement, using what little strength she had to add momentum.

Morgan stepped back, but the counter prevented her from going any further. As she leaned away, razor blades on the tip of the cane arced toward her face.

*   *   *

Down in the basement, Henry Palarae stepped in front of the light with a crossbow in his hands. It had a slender steel frame with a spring-loaded stock, and if Jake hadn't been on the wrong end of it, he might have appreciated the weapon.

He decided that now would be a good time to spark up a conversation.

"I can get you some nice fresh corpses for your art if that's what you're looking for?"

Palarae smiled as he reached for a bolt, the sharp metal tip glinting in the light. "The dead I seek are more than mere bodies, for they will become saints." He looked up and Jake saw a spark of excitement in the man's eyes, an anticipation of the pleasure ahead. "The relics I create must be worthy of taking their place in history."

Palarae fixed the bolt and pulled back the string, notching it ready to fire. The crossbow required little skill to use, especially when the target was shackled to the ground. There was no way he could miss at this distance.

"What saint will I become?" Jake asked, trying to keep Palarae engaged. "I'd love to see what you intend. After all, I won't be able to appreciate the finished product."

Palarae hesitated a moment before placing the crossbow down on the floor, the bolt aimed slightly to one side. He reached back around the light and pulled out a book of paintings marked by a piece of worn leather. The jeweler opened the book and turned it around so Jake could see a particular image.

A muscular young man stood bound to a pillar, his gaze fixed on heaven while behind him lay the ruins of an ancient city. The man's face was contorted with pain, his body pierced by arrows as blood dripped from his wounds.

"Saint Sebastian," Palarae said. "This particular painting is by Andrea Mantegna, a fifteenth-century artist. I saw it once on a research trip to the Louvre and it stayed with me." He walked closer and ran a fingertip over Jake's muscled torso. "Sebastian was a Praetorian Guard, one of the elite. When you came into the shop, I saw military experience in your posture and the vision of Sebastian came to mind."

"So he was killed by arrows?"

Palarae shook his head. "No, that was merely the beginning. He was shot many times and then beaten to death." He met Jake's gaze. "But for my purposes, the crossbow bolts will be enough."

Jake looked down at the picture. "Maybe you can start with one in the leg and work up?"

Palarae chuckled. "That was my plan. I've given you a cocktail of drugs to heighten sensation and I'll photograph you as we proceed, as well as doing some preliminary sketches. My knowledge of human anatomy has progressed well since I began my work on the saints, so I'll make it last."

As his captor walked back to the light, Jake scanned the room for anything he could use to get out of here.

If he could just unhook himself.

He sagged down as far as he could and then pushed off the floor, trying to leap and twist off whatever held him above. The chains rattled, and he writhed and bucked, desperation rising as he realized he was held fast. Jake panted as he slumped back against the restraints.

Palarae watched his exertions with a raised eyebrow. "You won't be getting out of here, so why not embrace your beatification? After all, few people get to become a saint and your bones, perhaps even your flesh, will be part of history."

"So you have a buyer lined up already?" Jake tried desperately to keep him talking.

"Enough." Palarae picked up the crossbow and cocked the bolt once more, the metallic click deadened by the stone walls.

He raised it up high and sighted down the stock.

Jake stared at the bolt pointed at his chest, imagining the thud of that tip into his heart. The first shot might not kill him, but it wouldn't take many more.

Palarae dipped the crossbow and fired.

Jake heard the dull crack of the shot before the bolt struck him in the upper thigh.

A second of shock, then agony lanced through him.

He sagged against the chains as his leg buckled, groaning and sucking in air as he tried to breathe through the burn.

Palarae snapped photos, crossbow hanging at his side as he captured the suffering of his victim.

Jake couldn't help the rage that surged inside, pain fueling his desire to pound the man into the stone floor and use the crossbow to turn the jeweler into one of his own saints. He pushed off his uninjured leg and rattled the chains, roaring as he tried once more to escape his bonds.

But his efforts sent more shards of agony shooting up his leg.

Palarae smiled as he took more photos. "Yes, fight it. I'll

capture the wounded animal in you, battling the pain of death even as it inevitably takes you."

"I'll give you a battle if you let me off this hook." Jake channelled his fury into white hot focus. There was a way out of here. He just had to find it.

Palarae lifted the crossbow once more.

*　*　*

Razor blades slashed the air in front of Morgan's face, the cane whistling as it flashed by. The old woman was surprisingly fast, the loose smock allowing her freedom of movement as she advanced, using the cane as a weapon.

Morgan stepped forward into the next swing, raising her arm to block the assault as the cane smashed down. In any other fight, she would have gone on the offensive by now, but some misguided respect for age prevented her.

"Ty kurwo!" the old woman spat as she swung the cane once more, kicking out with heavy boots at the same time. Morgan didn't know any Polish, but the curse words needed no translation.

She didn't have time for this. If the mother was so inclined to violence, then she didn't want to leave Jake in the hands of the son for much longer.

Morgan jumped over the counter and grabbed a crucifix from the wall, the metal heavy in her hand. As the old woman swung the cane again, Morgan used the crucifix to slam the weapon down, pinning it to the counter-top.

The old woman let go and rushed toward the back of the shop, clearly going for another weapon. But age and the flap of her smock hampered her movements.

Morgan dived for the old woman's legs and took her down, rolling slightly to minimize harm, the memory of the kibbutzim fresh in her mind. This was a fight she needed to win, but she didn't want to add to the old woman's suffering.

"Nie powstrzymasz go. Wykonuje pracę Boga." The old woman kept up her stream of Polish as Morgan pinned her limbs down and turned her over, face down to the floor.

With one hand holding the old woman's arms, Morgan dragged her assailant into the back office out of sight of anyone walking past. She hoisted the cursing, spitting woman onto a chair and used a roll of packing tape to secure her limbs, putting a final piece over her mouth to dampen the torrent of abuse.

Despite the unusual turn of events, Morgan was encouraged. Jake must be here. She went to the front door and locked it to prevent anyone else from entering, and on the way back through the shop; she picked up the razor-tipped cane. Morgan had trained in the martial art of Krav Maga when she served in the Israel Defense Force. One of its key principles was to use any weapon at hand, and this was a pretty good staff.

As she walked to the basement door, the old woman howled into her gag. A sound of frustration. A mother trying to warn her son.

Morgan pushed the door open and descended.

CHAPTER 11

JAKE BRACED HIMSELF AS Palarae's finger tightened on the trigger once more, the jeweler's eyes bright, his mouth slightly open in anticipation of the torture to come.

A sudden thud came from above, then the faint sounds of struggle.

Palarae frowned, and the head of the crossbow dipped a little as he tilted his head to listen.

Morgan. It must be.

But she wouldn't know what weapon Palarae held and Jake couldn't bear the thought of that bolt striking home in her flesh. He would take the pain himself before letting Morgan be hurt. He had to give her time to reach him — and he needed Palarae to loose that bolt.

Jake rattled his chains, pushing out his broad chest against the bonds to present a target.

"I'm ready for another."

Palarae raised the crossbow again. "Quiet!"

But Jake didn't stop with the jangling of his metallic restraints, every movement masking the sound from upstairs.

Palarae took two steps across the floor of the basement, his face contorted with rage. He rammed the hilt of the crossbow into Jake's solar plexus with brutal force.

Jake gasped for breath, unable to double over as he sagged from his bonds.

The sounds drew closer. Footsteps in the room above.

Palarae crouched like a hunter, raising the crossbow as he eased open the door and headed up the stairs on silent feet. He had all the advantages of knowing the terrain, and the man was clearly an experienced killer.

Jake tried desperately to suck in some breath, anything to fuel his voice.

"Morgan!" he croaked, and then a little louder. "Morgan!"

But there was nothing he could do to stop Palarae, and Jake could only imagine the sharp tip of the crossbow bolt slamming into Morgan's body.

*　*　*

Morgan descended the narrow wooden staircase from the office. The steps creaked under her feet as she stepped down carefully; the cane raised and ready for attack. A green light shone from below and the musty smell of old books wafted up along with the sharp tang of metalwork in progress. She couldn't sense anyone in the room ahead, but then the old woman's curses were loud enough even through her gag to disguise any sound.

Aware that she would be framed in the doorway as she stepped into the room, Morgan ran down the last few steps. She ducked and rolled at the bottom, presenting a moving target as she found shelter behind a large armchair.

No shots came, no sound or even a response to her arrival.

She peered out from behind the chair and looked around the room. Fitted shelving filled with books flanked an over-sized desk where the equipment of the jeweler lay ready for use. Sharp edges of files and diamond-tipped cutters glinted in the light next to a heavy sketchbook, its pages lay open to display the clean lines of a man's body.

Morgan couldn't quite make out the detail so she ran across to the desk in a crouch, pulling the sketchbook to the floor as she sheltered behind the thick wooden table legs. The man in the drawing was perfectly proportioned, his muscle tone outlined with the strokes of someone intimately acquainted with human anatomy. His face was contorted with pain from the arrows piercing his skin, but Morgan could still recognize Jake beneath the agony.

She could not let this sketch become reality.

There was only one other door in the room. It must lead to wherever the jeweler prepared his art.

Morgan stood and grasped the sketchbook in both hands, leaving the razor-tipped cane behind as it was less useful in close-quarter fighting. Her heart beat faster with the anticipation of violence and she let her anger rise as she strode to the door. Palarae must be down there, but she would not underestimate him as she had his mother.

Morgan stood to one side of the door and turned the handle slowly. It opened with a soft click.

As the crack opened, she heard Jake calling her name.

She ducked into the open doorway, a feint designed to draw Palarae out, then quickly drew back again.

A crossbow bolt thudded into the doorframe, missing her by an inch.

With no hesitation, Morgan hurtled down the stairs, rushing the jeweler, hoping it wasn't an automatic crossbow. This was her only chance.

Palarae stood at the bottom, his attention on reloading. He glanced up as Morgan darted down, a silent Fury, a goddess of vengeance.

She rammed the jeweler, using the sketchbook to shove him back into the basement.

He smashed into a massive light rig and fell backward,

dropping the crossbow. Morgan followed him down, strad-dling him, pinning his arms with her legs as he writhed beneath her.

The jeweler screamed as she hammered his face with the sketchbook. Its sharp edges carved deep furrows into his skin, knocking Palarae senseless as his blood soaked the rigid ivory paper.

Morgan kept pounding until he fell silent, then she reached for the discarded crossbow, turning it around to use the blunt end as a club. Her breath came fast, her vision narrowed only to the bloodied face of the jeweler.

She raised the crossbow, ready for the final blow.

"Morgan." Jake's voice filtered through the haze of blood-lust. "Wait. We need him."

His words stopped her, even though she wanted to hammer the weapon down and crush Palarae's skull. Morgan slowed her breathing, returning from a place of darkness that stank of blood and suffering, a void that could consume her if she allowed it to. When those she loved were threatened, Morgan knew she was capable of anything.

"It's OK, he's out," Jake said softly. "Help me down from here."

Morgan threw the crossbow into a far corner and clam-bered off the jeweler, pushing down her rage as she took in the scene.

Jake hung from chains, wearing only a pair of green boxer shorts, his feet shackled to the ground. His muscular chest was a match for Palarae's sketch, and a crossbow bolt pierced his leg, blood trickling from the wound.

"Nice timing." Jake grinned, the corkscrew scar twisting away from his eyebrow. "Although ten minutes earlier would have been preferable."

Morgan strode over, relieved by his wisecracks, even though she knew his leg must be agony. "I stopped for a *slivovitz* on the way over. Didn't want you to think I was worried."

As she stood close to Jake's shackled body, Morgan wanted to wrap her arms around him. There was so much unsaid between them and, to be honest, she had imagined his naked chest pressed against hers, but this was hardly how she'd pictured it.

She pressed the button on the hydraulic hoist and lowered him down. Jake took his weight on his uninjured leg while Morgan unhooked his hands and helped him to a chair.

She knelt down in front of him, focusing on the wound in his leg rather than his semi-naked muscular frame. The crossbow bolt was lodged deep. "You need proper medical attention. I can't deal with this myself with whatever basic first aid supplies we can find."

Jake nodded, his face pale with shock. "Sorry I can't help with Palarae, but I trust you'll find out where the relics might be. If I get some good drugs, I'll be ready by the time you figure out where we're going next."

He looked down at his almost naked body and grinned up at her. "Any chance you can find me a shirt or something?"

Morgan flushed a little and stood up to look for something other than the scraps of fabric on the floor. "I saw a coat rack upstairs. Don't go anywhere."

She darted back up to the workroom and grabbed one of Palarae's trench coats and the razor-tipped cane, taking them back down to Jake.

"Just don't wave this around at the hospital or they'll get a nasty shock."

He hobbled up the stairs, leaning on the cane while Morgan ran up to the shop in front of him and called Martin Klein, ignoring the muffled cries of the old woman.

Morgan explained the situation and by the time Jake made it up to the entrance, the flashing blue lights of a private ambulance came from the cobbled streets beyond.

As a paramedic wheeled a gurney toward them, Jake reached for Morgan's arm. His face was pale with pain, but his amber-flecked eyes were set with determination.

"Don't go without me."

She hesitated a moment and then nodded. They had managed missions while injured before. They could do it again. "I'll find out where we're heading. I'm sure the jeweler will be happy to tell me now."

Jake lay back on the gurney, and within a minute, the ambulance was speeding away. Morgan was grateful for ARKANE's contacts all over the world and she knew he was in the best hands. It left her free to deal with Palarae and after seeing what he'd done to Jake, perhaps the jeweler needed a taste of his own medicine.

She went back into the shop and past the little office. The old woman had fallen silent, her eyes wary, like an animal whose instinct drives them to stillness in the presence of a stronger predator. Morgan retraced her footsteps back to the workshop and then further down into the basement.

Henry Palarae lay unconscious on his back, his face bloody, lit by the powerful photography lights he'd set up for his macabre reenactment of Saint Sebastian's torture. The bent and broken sketchbook lay next to him, the pages stained crimson. Fragments of Jake's clothing littered the floor by the shackles that had restrained him, and Morgan wondered how many others had suffered in this room.

While part of her wanted to enact appropriate judgment for Palarae, Morgan knew there were crimes he needed to answer for. The police would tear this place up looking for evidence once they knew about the fake relics. She would hand this whole thing over to Director Marietti and he could facilitate the next steps, but right now, she needed to find out who had the Becket reliquary and the bones of the Magi.

She looked down at Palarae. His breath rasped through a broken and bloody nose, and bruises already formed around his eyes. The heavy sketchbook had been a remarkably effective weapon and Morgan appreciated his dedication to quality art materials.

Right now, the jeweler was of no use to her. He was out cold and would probably emerge with concussion. However, Palarae was organized and meticulous in his art, so perhaps he would be similar in his record-keeping.

Morgan returned to the workshop and searched the shelving for invoices related to the business. She pulled out boxes of paperwork going back years, rifling through them for any sign of the fake reliquaries. They were truly precious works of art in themselves, so the payments must have been substantial.

After hunting in several boxes, she found a slim folder containing sketches of the Becket reliquary and other similar projects, the pencil lines drawn with Palarae's distinctive style. Between the pages, there was an invoice made out to Dr. Kelley Montague-Breton.

Morgan smiled as she traced the name with a fingertip. Once Martin Klein set his algorithms on her, the woman would have nowhere to hide.

CHAPTER 12

Northumberland, England

As the winter sunlight faded to dusk the next day, Morgan drove through a landscape that couldn't be more different from the medieval heart of Kraków.

Northumberland had a history of invasion from the Romans and the Angles, to the Danes and the Normans, and the eternal battles between the Scots and the English, whose conflict still echoed in modern times. It was a wild place with a sparse population where rugged hills and moorland hid valleys of ancient woods. Shades of dull rust tinged the clouds above, like bloodstains upon the sky. A result of some pollutant rising in the air, no doubt, but Morgan couldn't shake the lingering feeling of dread as they drove further north.

Jake sat in the passenger seat beside her, fueled by pain-killers, his wounded leg bandaged under his jeans. Neither of them were strangers to pain and injury sustained on missions and Morgan trusted he would be at her side whatever lay ahead — limping, for sure, but they had managed with worse. Jake scrolled through his phone, reading notes on Dr. Kelley Montague-Breton that outlined her public persona as

CEO of Breton Biomedical, her connections to the cadaver trade, and her private visits to the estate they drove toward. Martin had discovered helicopter flight plans indicating she would arrive in Northumberland today, perhaps to take delivery of the bones of the Magi. They would make sure she had an appropriate welcome.

"This estate has been in her family for generations," Jake said. "The financials of Breton Biochemical are also entwined with Anchorite Holdings, which has links to government and a web of companies going back hundreds of years." He frowned down at the notes. "There are also references to the Black Anchorite. Some kind of figurehead, perhaps? There are no photos, but conspiracy websites claim the estate has links to the occult."

Morgan swerved around a bend, shifting gears and speeding away as they drove uphill toward a dense forest on the edge of an escarpment. "Relics and the occult are certainly an interesting hobby for the CEO of a biomedical company, but body parts are body parts, I guess, no matter how old they are."

She switched her lights to full beam as the forest canopy closed in overhead, blocking out the last rays of the sun. The trees were dense on either side of the road, but now and then a view opened up of the deep crevasse to one side with jagged rocks and a rushing river below.

Morgan was used to the soft green and welcoming woods of the south of England, tamed by generations into clean lines and bounded by neat stone walls. Up here the land was wild and in this forest, the tree branches loomed over them with seeming malevolence. The dark limbs twisted overhead and crowded the edge of the road, leaving them no path of escape. It seemed as if the trees were not separate things, but part of a single organism that ruled this domain, pressing down upon them and turning dusk into night. Their leaves were mottled and pockmarked with black poisonous sacs like the slimy skin of a toad, and the smell of the forest was more like dank moldering meat than the expected fresh scent of pine needles after rain.

"Locals say there's a curse on this forest," Jake said. "Those who walk here find their limbs softening until they sink to the forest floor and the land devours them, dissolving their flesh into mulch." He looked out the window. "No doubt a legend spread to keep people away from the estate."

"No doubt." Morgan heard the hesitancy in her own voice as she wound up the window to shut out the smell. She concentrated on the road, which narrowed as it headed up the escarpment and the forest clustered even closer.

A flash of silver struck the trees as the headlights caught something moving to one side.

Morgan frowned and feathered the brakes, suddenly aware of shadows shifting between the gnarled trunks. Wild dogs hunting in a pack, keeping pace with the car as rising moonlight glinted on silver fur and sharp teeth.

"I see them. Just keep driving." Jake's voice was calm even as he reached around into the back seat and pulled open the heavy case Martin had provided. Two pistols, plenty of ammunition. Knives and climbing gear.

An enormous beast suddenly darted out in front of the car.

In the headlights, Morgan glimpsed misshapen muscled haunches and an oversized powerful jaw that could rip off a limb within a heartbeat.

She braked lightly and swerved around it.

The car skidded, tires shrieking on the road as they spun around, fishtailing as she fought for control.

Jake held his gun ready to engage, but in her rearview mirror, Morgan saw something even bigger step out of the gloom. Its sleek black coat shimmered like oil, tight on powerful muscled limbs tipped with claws that trailed the dirt of the forest behind it.

This was an ancient creature, bred as a weapon.

It snarled, revealing yellow teeth with scraps of flesh between. Behind it, more creatures gathered, shadows upon shadows.

They would have no chance if they stepped out of the car.

"Hold on." Morgan gripped the steering wheel and pressed the accelerator, pushing the car to its limit as they sped up the hill.

The creatures gave chase, loping after their prey as they howled in a feral sound of violent joy in the hunt.

The twisted trees closed around them, but up ahead, Morgan thought the shadows grew lighter. A break in the forest, perhaps? She accelerated toward it as the pack closed in, foamy lather dripping from their sharp teeth as they snapped at the rear wheels.

The dense green forest ended abruptly in a short tarmac drive in front of a pair of gigantic iron gates. They blocked the road ahead, flanked by towering stone walls and a sheer drop to one side down the cliff.

Morgan braked hard, and they skidded to a halt only millimeters from the metal barrier.

The feral pack bayed for blood behind them.

Morgan reached behind for the comfort of her SP-21 Barak pistol, her hand tight around the weapon. If the creatures surrounded them, she and Jake would have little choice but to fight.

But the beasts stayed within the shadows of the forest, their territory bounded by the trees. Minutes later, they disappeared, and the forest fell silent in their wake. No birdsong, no crack of branches, only the eerie sound of wind rushing up the escarpment.

Jake exhaled slowly. "That was fun."

Morgan opened the door and climbed out, her body flushed with the adrenalin of the chase. A carpet of dry leaves lay underfoot, cracking and crunching like the breaking of tiny bones as she walked over to the metal barrier.

The gates were fashioned with filigree letters entwined with images of castle turrets. Weathered stone pillars stood on either side carved with medieval longswords, while above them loomed creatures of legend, part lion, part serpent, with open jaws and blank eyes. Lichen covered each one with patches of green and yellow, like living skin on dead stone. A gigantic wall made of enormous blocks barred the way either side of the gate, cracked and fissured with the ravages of time, but standing unbowed against the elements.

Jake joined Morgan in front of the gate. "This looks like it hasn't been opened for centuries. Do you think Martin's intel might be wrong about the place?"

Morgan shook her head. "There must be another way in."

She reached out and grasped the metal — then pulled back quickly. It was so cold that her flesh would fuse to it if she held on too long, slivers of skin ripping away to leave bloody wounds.

Jake leaned his weight against the gates, pushing hard, but they didn't move.

Morgan looked up at the thick ivy twisted amongst the filigree letters with sturdy branches and deformed leaves, anchoring the metal so it was part of the land.

"Think you can manage a climb?"

"Last one over buys the beers."

Morgan laughed as Jake hobbled to the car, exaggerating his limp as he pulled the bag from the back seat. Martin's images of the estate had led them to expect some difficulty, so they'd packed climbing axes and ropes, but this ancient wall had plenty of broken masonry for footholds and the thick winding branches of ivy would be easy enough to navigate.

As Jake filled a smaller pack with items they might need, Morgan clambered up the side of the wall, relishing the tension in her muscles as she climbed. She paused at the top, crouching down behind a crenellation to peer into the estate beyond.

An apple orchard with gnarled mature trees stretched out toward a jumble of buildings. An ancient citadel with stark walls and slit windows stood in the middle, surrounded by structures from different periods, including a modern guard tower and a helipad where a helicopter sat waiting.

Jake climbed up beside her. "I vote we use that later and avoid our friends in the forest."

"Seconded." Morgan pointed at the guard tower and then down at a ring of cameras with blinking green lights. "But we might have company soon. They must know we're here."

They clambered down the other side of the wall and walked through the orchard, the twisted trunks evidence of how long the trees had provided for the estate. But nothing grew upon the path that wound toward the citadel. Where tendrils of the wild forest outside the gates had broken through the tarmac in an unstoppable march of life, something in the ancient stone held them back here. The roots of the apple trees nearest the path were blackened, curling back on themselves in a cage of twisted branches.

There was no one waiting as they entered the boundaries of the buildings, so they kept walking toward the citadel. It wasn't the biggest structure in the compound, but it exuded a dark gravitational pull, as if everything orbited around it, a fortress from medieval times that retained its imposing military strength. The relics would be held at the heart of the place, and Morgan knew they had to get inside.

She looked up to the slit windows, slivers of black opening into the dark heart of the building. Something waited in there, something that drove nature to turn away in horror. She gripped her gun more tightly and walked on.

As they entered the courtyard in front of the citadel, security guards stepped out from shadowed doorways.

The leader had bulging muscles that stretched his uniform and a face that was mightily improved by the balaclava they'd last seen him in. He held a metal bar in one hand.

"Didn't think you'd make it through the forest, but don't worry, we're sending you back out there." He thumped the metal bar against his other palm and grinned. "After we've had a little fun."

Five other men stepped out to join him, three with guns and two more with metal bars, cruel smiles on their lips.

CHAPTER 13

As Jake tensed next to her, Morgan shifted her position. They stood back to back, sighting the security guards down the barrel of their guns. She knew they could take down at least three of the men, but they were outnumbered and the leader knew it.

"If you surrender now, you'll have a chance with the dogs in the forest." He hefted the weight of the metal bar. "I'll even give you this after I've finished."

Morgan felt Jake lean back against her a little, his weight shifting. She knew her partner. He was in no mood to let these men anywhere near.

So be it.

Morgan readied herself, her target on one guard holding an automatic. These men might be ex-military, but it was likely a while since they'd been in an actual fight.

She prepared to fire.

"Stop!" A woman's voice rang out across the courtyard.

The leader held up his fist, stopping his men from attacking. Morgan considered firing first to take advantage of the pause, but then Dr. Kelley Montague-Breton emerged from the shadows.

She was petite in stature, but her authority was clear as the men stepped back to let her pass. She walked in front of the guns and assessed the scene. There were dark shadows under her clear eyes and a depth of pain that seemed unusual for such a wealthy heiress and powerful CEO.

Morgan kept her gun raised, aware that everything could change in a second. "We're here for the Becket reliquary and the bones of the Magi."

"And whatever else you have hidden here," Jake added. "ARKANE will have a team up here soon to investigate what the hell you've been doing."

Kelley laughed softly and shook her head. "You have no idea who you're dealing with. Your Director Marietti will find only obstacles and those in power will pressure ARKANE to close any investigation. Anchorite is untouchable."

Morgan knew she wasn't bluffing. Martin's notes had implied Anchorite was bound deep into the corridors of government and its power went back generations. It held the kind of influence that remained in the shadows, but could wield both immense wealth or a silent blade as required.

Kelley paced the courtyard, assessing Morgan and Jake with a cool gaze. After a moment, she stopped, her posture changing as if she'd come to a decision. "There is no way for you to reach Anchorite through official channels. But perhaps you can end a cycle that I can't finish myself."

She looked up at the citadel. "The Black Anchorite has ruled my family for generations, tied by history and sustained by blood. I've tried to end it, but he..." Her words trailed off and in the silence, Morgan sensed years of dread.

Kelley took a deep breath and turned to the leader of the security guards. "Let them in, Zale."

Zale frowned, confusion flickering over his features. "But we have to protect the citadel." He looked up at the looming stone tower and lowered his voice to a whisper. "What if they don't make it? He will demand a sacrifice."

Kelley reached out and touched his arm. "There has already been so much sacrifice, far more than you know. I have to take this chance — for my sons, for future genera-tions. For me." She leaned in and spoke softly. "Please. Let them try."

Zale softened at her touch and Morgan could see there was something between them, even if it had yet to blossom.

He waved his men away. "Back to your stations. I'll handle this."

The other guards returned inside the buildings and Zale turned, determination on his face. "I'm going in, too."

Kelley frowned. "Why? Let them take the risk. You don't know what he's capable of."

Zale shook off her hand and turned to look up at the citadel. "Every time you stepped through that door, I wanted to come with you and help end him. This is my chance." He gripped her hands. "Let me prove myself to you."

A sudden chill wind blew over the escarpment, sweeping a tornado of dead leaves up from the orchard. They whirled in the air, twisting into shapes of ruined corpses that reached out with undead hands. As the smell of rot and decay per-meated the courtyard, the cry of a crow pierced the air, then many more joined the harsh chorus. Morgan looked up to see a flock of dark birds wheeling above, calling what could have been a warning. Was it for them or for whoever lay within?

"You must hurry," Kelley said. "Or he will have time to prepare, and remember, things may not be as they seem inside. Stay together."

Morgan gazed up at the citadel, black stones against a darkening sky as carrion crows circled above. Perhaps a temporary truce was the best way forward until they made it out with the relics and dealt with this Black Anchorite, whatever he might be. She and Jake had faced all manner of adversaries on their missions, and Morgan was ready for this one. As long as Jake was by her side, they could manage whatever might come.

She glanced at Jake, and he nodded in agreement. Together, they fell in behind the security guard.

Zale stepped up to the door of the citadel and bent his head for a moment as if he prayed for strength, then he put his hand against the thick wood studded by iron rivets. It seemed impregnable, but as he pushed the door, it swung open silently. The dark maw of a corridor stretched away before them.

The crows fell silent above and the whirling leaves fell to the stones of the courtyard. Zale held his gun out and stepped warily inside, Morgan and Jake right behind him, weapons high.

The temperature dropped inside the stone walls and a sudden bone-chilling cold made Morgan shiver as the door swung shut behind them. Motes of dust and ash rose from the floor, hanging in the air and clinging to their clothes as they walked on. The flagstones of the corridor were uneven, some half-sunken into the ground, and scuttling insects burrowed blindly in the cracks between as they hid away from the light. It smelled of the aftermath of battle — smoke and blood and fear. A memory of violence sunk deep into the citadel, woven into the fabric of stone and earth beneath.

There were places where the veil was thin, where the line blurred between the living and the dead, the present and other times. Morgan had brushed against such places before on ARKANE missions, but this citadel was peculiar. Time was confused here, its hold on the fabric of life somehow suspended.

An oversized crucifix hung on one wall lit from below, the body of Christ tortured and bloody, his face transfixed in pain, his eyes pleading for release from two thousand years hanging on the tree. But even though the citadel had the trappings of faith, Morgan sensed that no prayers had been spoken here for generations. The air seemed heavy with curses overlaid with a cloying incense that couldn't hide its dark nature.

"Welcoming place, isn't it?" The heavy stone around them dampened Jake's soft words, but Morgan allowed a flicker of a smile to play over her lips. Her ARKANE partner was thankfully irrepressible, even when injured. Perhaps she needed some of those painkillers…

Zale stopped at another heavy door at the end of the corridor, this one etched with faded runes mingled with medieval curses. The door handle was sculpted steel crafted from the rolled blades of vanquished enemies. Morgan and Jake readied their weapons as Zale reached out with a shaking hand.

Before he could touch it, the door opened with a creak.

An old woman stood in the doorway, her eyes opaque as she stared into the air above their heads. Her skin was dry and cracked, shrunken against her bones.

"He's expecting you," she croaked with a ragged breath.

She waved them on and as Morgan walked past; the woman looked right at her. The irises in her blind eyes seemed to swirl into patterns of storm clouds where deformed winged creatures flew, talons outstretched, as they hunted their prey in the shadows.

A long hallway stretched in front of them with tapestries hung on both sides, the rich fibers coated with a layer of dust. As they walked past, Morgan recognized the sack of Jerusalem by Crusaders underneath the grime. Knights mounted on horses with red crosses on their armor slashed down at infidels and pilgrims alike, their faces contorted with lust for blood and glory. Heaped bodies lay at the base of the tapestries, each face a portrait of suffering, while maggots squirmed out of bloody wounds and carrion birds pecked at eyes and exposed flesh. A banner of embroidered words hung above the killing field: *God will know his own.*

The images were so vivid that Morgan thought she could hear the cries of Crusaders ring out across the battlefield, the clash of metal, the thud of horses' hooves, the screams of the dying. It was as if they were in the midst of battle, the smell of smoke from fires, the stench of blood and voided bowels, the sweat of men and horses as they slaughtered in the name of God.

The cacophony grew louder. The battle was almost upon them, sound and sensation intensifying into a crescendo.

The corridor grew hazy and the tapestries writhed with life. Morgan fell to her knees, overwhelmed with memories of war. She was under fire in the Golan Heights, a soldier in the Israel Defense Force, fighting to stay alive. A flash of light and her husband, Elian, died once more in a hail of bullets, his blood coating her hands, soaking into her uniform.

The bullets came again — over and over — and still, she couldn't save him. Tears rolled down her cheeks as Morgan cradled Elian's broken body against her own, another pointless death in an endless war.

The sounds of battle rolled around her in waves, emanating from the tapestries, along with memories of death by fire and torture, bullet and knife, fist and boot. Memories that weren't hers anymore, but somehow projected from the surrounding walls.

In the depths of the bloody vision, Morgan clawed her way back to the surface, mentally setting aside the past. She had faced such horrors before and lived. The memories couldn't touch her now.

She placed one hand on the carpet, anchoring herself to the physical world, pushing away the swirling vortex of terror as she fought to escape the strange visions that the citadel projected into their minds. Beside her, Jake reached out for a tapestry with an expression of anguish, tears on his cheeks. Did he see the broken bodies of his family there?

Zale stumbled and put his hands over his ears. "Make it stop," he moaned. He fell to his knees and bent forward, his head almost touching the carpet as he tried to block out the assault on his senses.

They had to get out of this corridor. There was something in the tapestries or in the air that dragged them into the violent depths of war. But Morgan would not turn back. It wasn't just the mission anymore. A dark curiosity led her on. She wanted to face the Black Anchorite.

She shook Jake's arm. "We need to move. Now!"

He blinked, confusion on his face, but as Morgan grabbed Zale under one arm, Jake took the other side. Together, they dragged the moaning security guard onward, through another door at the end of the corridor, and stumbled into the heart of the citadel.

A circular room opened up to a skylight high above, with stone walls bounded by plain Gothic arches. Each led off to separate rooms, most stacked high with books. A mottled rug of black and crimson, the colors of pitch and blood, led toward a fireplace roaring with flame, although somehow the room remained piercingly cold. A gigantic oil painting of the End Times hung on the wall. Demons boiled from the pit of hell, tormenting the damned with spiked claws and sharp teeth, ripping flesh from bone as an uncaring god turned his back on them all.

A robed figure stood looking up at the painting, his stature tall and commanding, a hood over his face. He turned as Morgan and Jake burst in and the firelight flickered over his ravaged face.

CHAPTER 14

THE BLACK ANCHORITE DREW back his hood. "Welcome to the citadel."

His words barely registered as Morgan stared at his ruined visage. His skin was loose against his skull, a patchwork of different hues, as if each pinch of flesh came from a separate corpse in varying stages of decomposition. Some were finely stitched together with the skilled hand of a surgeon, perhaps Kelley herself, whereas others were sutured with broad dark thread that rose in lumps around open sores that wept pus and blood.

His breath wheezed in and out, almost a death rattle, as he held the edge of the fireplace with an arthritic clawed hand, seams of broken skin visible on the exposed flesh.

Zale moaned and as Morgan helped Jake lower him to the ground, everything finally clicked into place. The stolen reliquaries, the links with the biomedical company, the stitched skin. The Black Anchorite was sustained by grafted body parts — a Frankenstein of holy relics, powered by a dark religion.

Morgan remembered how the golem at the Gates of Hell had been enlivened by words of faith. Given the amount of power that religious relics were believed to hold, perhaps they could indeed sustain a body — but for how long?

The Black Anchorite coughed and flecks of yellow pus streaked with blood landed on the carpet in front of him. He licked his cracked lips with a thick tongue of mottled purple and, despite his ancient appearance, there was something predatory in his gaze.

He pointed down at Zale, the security guard now curled on the ground with his hands over his ears, still moaning softly, lost in a battle he couldn't escape.

"You have brought me fresh harvest, for which I am grateful. His blood will aid the transplantation of the bones of the Magi."

Morgan tried to raise her gun, but a miasma of smoke and despair rippled out of the battle corridor, surrounding them with mist. It weakened her and made the weapon seem too heavy. She leaned against a stone pillar as beside her, Jake dropped to his knees then crumpled to the floor, his face contorted with nightmares.

In the haze, the Black Anchorite moved faster than Morgan expected, or perhaps her experience of time shifted somehow. One minute he was by the fireplace and the next, he plucked the gun from her hand, his ruined face close to hers.

"You don't need that here, Morgan Sierra, agent of ARKANE. But there is a way you can save your friends."

Morgan felt no surprise at his words of recognition. She and Jake had spent many missions searching for relics, some of them currently resting in the vault under Trafalgar Square, some returned to their places of worship. It wasn't surprising that the Black Anchorite knew of them. It was much more concerning that he had not been on their radar until now.

He threw the gun into the misty shadows and then held out his hand, the weeping sores and stitched pieces of flesh stretching as he waved more billowing smoke over Jake and Zale. Morgan could only watch helplessly, her strength gone, as they disappeared from view into the haze of bloody memory.

The Black Anchorite turned toward her and waved his hand again, the air shimmering around them as his face changed. The ravages of time dropped away and Morgan glimpsed a middle-aged knight with patrician features, his expression etched with a mixture of ambition and regret as he looked out across a war-ravaged landscape.

Smoke eddied around them once more and he was back to an abomination.

"The lines between the ages are blurred here," the Black Anchorite wheezed. "You see me as I once was."

"Who are you?" Morgan whispered.

The Black Anchorite sighed. "I was William de Tracy back then, cursed for doing the bidding of my king. After striking down the rebel Archbishop Thomas Becket with my fellow knights, we were exiled to Jerusalem to fight in the Crusader wars. For many years, I searched for a way back and then, in a ruined desert temple, I found the heart."

He pulled open the front of his robe, exposing his chest. A blackened husk of an organ lay in the center of mottled skin with dark veins curling into what remained of his flesh like some parasitic creature from the depths.

"I have borne it for over eight hundred years and before it lived through me, there were other lifetimes." The Black Anchorite stared into the smoke, as if gazing into another realm. "I see memories that are not mine. A temple in ancient Egypt as embalmers conjured dark magic into the organs of a king. A desert sacrifice where eternal life was given as a reward for the soul of a princess." He shook his head. "But the past matters not, only the future."

He walked slowly along the carpet back to the fireplace and Morgan felt compelled to follow him, the tendrils of smoke swirling about her, pushing her forward. She glanced back, but Jake was hidden, her partner smothered under the thick miasma. She could only hope he still breathed and could pull himself out of the nightmare visions before it was too late.

Demons from the painting of the End Times looked down upon them as the Black Anchorite reached out to stroke Morgan's cheek. She shuddered as his rough, wet fingers touched her skin, but she didn't have the strength to flinch away.

"I've read about you, Morgan, and all the agents of ARKANE. I have followed your missions with interest and sent my own forces after the relics you discovered. You know how to fight, but you're not a soldier like the men with you. You're curious. A seeker. You have a deep thirst for knowledge — and for experience. Time is your enemy."

His words resonated deep within Morgan, a truth that few understood. The drive to learn new things pushed her into the labyrinth of ARKANE and the fragments of knowledge she gleaned along the way only heightened the exhilaration of their missions. Sometimes she could almost feel the gears spinning as her mind whirled faster than those around her, gathering insights that others missed.

It was hard to explain how perception emerged from experience, but the Black Anchorite understood. His hundreds of years of life gave him the wisdom she craved. His vast libraries of knowledge were testament to his continued desire to learn, but it was the generations of experience that made Morgan's head spin with possibility.

The Black Anchorite pointed to his ruined face. "You see this broken flesh, but there were lifetimes of strength and virility when my body didn't require the parts that sustain it now." He shook his head. "But it's not enough anymore. The heart requires a stronger body. Its power and memory must live on. So I ask you, seeker, do you want to live for hundreds of years? Do you want precious time to discover the secrets of the world?"

Morgan couldn't speak, she could hardly breathe.

His words hung in the air like a beautiful flower tainted with poison and part of her wanted to grasp it with both hands and drink in the scent of promise. What could she do with so much time? It would be a dark gift indeed, but she did not have to use it as the Black Anchorite had done. She could pursue a different path, a better path.

"Come." The Black Anchorite walked on through the smoke under an archway into what looked like a chapel. But as the haze shifted, Morgan saw ancient symbols etched into the stone walls — the Egyptian ankh, the Celtic knot, the ouroboros — all representing eternal life, sought after in every culture.

An obsidian altar stood at one end with a copper bowl on top, burning with a strange fire, adding to the smoke billowing around them with the scent of sandalwood. Next to the fire bowl, the relic of Thomas Becket and the bones of the Magi waited for their transplantation.

Before the altar, two stone slabs lay side by side engraved with the outline of human figures, each with a figure-of-eight infinity symbol in place of their hearts.

The Black Anchorite waved his hand toward one slab, and Morgan found herself longing to lie down upon it. She could rest there. It would cradle her, and the heaviness in her limbs would sink away into the stone.

The pull of dark promise encouraged her, and she climbed onto the slab, lying back with her head resting against the cool stone. Visions swirled around her, the places she could go and the experiences she could have in years ahead, turning the tiny chapel into an expansive future world.

"The relic comes with a promise — and a curse." The Black Anchorite gazed down at Morgan and intoned, "*From death comes life, but life is the price.* You will have many glorious years, but life is indeed a price when it goes on for so long. My world passed away and I have long forgotten everyone I loved. I sustained myself with relics but the veil parts more each day and I long to step into darkness. Now you are here, my time is over."

He sighed and clutched at his chest, stumbling a little as if the organ beat faster to punish his words. He ripped open the robe to expose the black heart, its surface oily with dark blood, the surrounding veins pulsing with life.

As Morgan looked up from the slab, the dark heart filled her vision. That pulsing of tainted blood sustained the Black Anchorite, the price of so many years of life.

His words echoed in her mind. His world had passed away, and hers would, too. Empires would rise and crumble. Jake, her sister Faye and even little Gemma would age and wither and die, and she would live on, their memories fading into nothing as the years passed. Even ARKANE's missions would seem petty and ephemeral against the backdrop of history.

Morgan's breath caught in her throat as she remembered sitting with her father in the hills above Safed in Israel one summer in a field of wildflowers. "For everything, there is a season," he said, quoting Ecclesiastes, his favorite Scripture. "A time to be born and a time to die. A time to grieve and a time to dance." He reached for her hand, and she could still feel his strong fingers in hers. "Dance while you can, Morgan, with the ones you love."

As her father's voice faded away, the Black Anchorite reached down and unzipped Morgan's jacket, pulling open the buttons of her shirt to reveal the skin of her chest above her sports bra.

She struggled desperately to free herself from the heavy smoke pressing down upon her, but tendrils wrapped around her wrists and ankles, snaking over her waist and binding her to the stone slab.

Above her, the Black Anchorite held the heart with both hands, closing his eyes as he pulled it away from his patchwork skin. He moaned as it ripped from him, the veins continuing to feed his flesh even as they stretched out toward its new host.

Black blood dripped from the dark organ onto Morgan's chest, stinging and burning her flesh. As the liquid sank into her skin, she glimpsed the heart's true nature. Corrupted by years of power and too much knowledge for anything human to bear, it would drive its host into dark delirium.

Life was indeed too much of a price.

Morgan writhed on the stone slab, her breath coming fast as she fought against the bonds of smoke. She couldn't let the organ touch her. She would be lost in its power within seconds.

The Black Anchorite finally wrenched the heart from his chest with a cry of loss. As he held it free from his body, regret rippled over his face as if he couldn't bear to be separated from his dark addiction.

In those seconds of hesitation, the smoke cleared a little, as if its power diminished when the shriveled organ had no host.

Morgan took her chance.

She bucked her hips and rolled out from under the Black Anchorite's outstretched arms, landing cat-like next to the slab.

She reached for the heart, wrenching it from the Black Anchorite's grasp even as he scrambled to keep hold of it. As its black blood pulsed over her skin like acid, Morgan threw it into the flaming fire on the altar.

"No!" The Black Anchorite's cry seemed to come from a thousand mouths, the lives of all those who hosted the cursed organ, who gave their limbs and blood to sustain its immortality.

He stumbled to the altar, reaching his withered fingers into the fire, but they crumbled into flakes and dropped in pieces to burn alongside the heart. The desiccated organ flared as it burst into life once more, then blackened and disintegrated into ash.

The Black Anchorite sank to his knees, collapsing against the altar and closing his eyes as his limbs crumbled beneath him. The smoke eddied and began to thin, its power dissipated with the end of the heart.

Morgan took a step forward, daring to hope that it was over.

The Black Anchorite opened his eyes once more, a dark stain turning them to corrupted blood. His gaze seemed to pierce Morgan's soul and as he reached out a shaking skeletal hand, something twisted inside her.

He was not the Black Anchorite anymore, but something far, far older.

"For what you have destroyed, you will suffer a blood torment that time can never heal…"

His lower jaw dropped open and thick black liquid dripped from his eyeballs like tar. His skin sloughed away, his bones crumbled and his robes collapsed as the body within broke apart, decaying to dust and fragments of bone amidst a pile of ragged cloth.

Morgan sank to her knees in front of the remains, her hand at her mouth as the cursed knight's final words echoed in her mind.

The smoke cleared in the chapel, and the sound of coughing came from the hall beyond. Jake stumbled out of the haze and knelt next to her.

He pulled Morgan into his arms. "He's gone. It's over."

But as the altar fire flickered out and the chill of the citadel pierced her deep inside, Morgan felt the truth of the Black Anchorite's curse tighten around her heart.

CHAPTER 15

Canterbury Cathedral, England. Two days later.

MORGAN STOOD BY A stone pillar in the nave as the song of the choir soared up to the vaulted roof above and onward to heaven. Twelve male choristers robed in purple sang psalms in praise of their God, each note disappearing in a moment even as their resonance lingered on.

Ancient stone, ancient faith, ancient songs. Morgan didn't believe as they did, but human voices in harmony were important in every faith. She closed her eyes and let the music transport her to the synagogue of her childhood, with her father as cantor, leading the faithful in prayer. But even that precious memory couldn't banish the echo of the curse spoken by the Black Anchorite in his final moments, the last gasp of an ancient creature that fought its end.

Morgan sighed and opened her eyes once more, the stark lines of the Gothic cathedral anchoring her to reality. The blood torment was promised as recompense for an act of destruction. An echo of the violence committed right here in the cathedral when the knights of Henry II struck down the Archbishop, his blood and brains soaking the hallowed ground. Perhaps returning the reliquary would be a step toward restitution.

She walked toward the chapel of Martyrdom, retracing her steps of just a few days ago.

The Dean stood in front of the Becket altar and turned as she entered, his face flooding with relief as he saw the reliquary in her hands.

"You have it. Thank God — and thank you, Morgan."

She handed it to him and he gently placed the precious object back in the glass box, removing the fake to make way for the real thing.

"The Pope will be here tomorrow. Perhaps you'd like to join us for the service?"

Morgan shook her head. "Thank you, but I need to get back to London. We have a lot of relics to sort through."

The Dean reached out and touched her arm. "You look haunted, like this mission still has a hold over you."

The expression in his kind eyes almost brought Morgan to tears as the words of the curse echoed in her mind.

"Can I pray for you?" the Dean continued.

After a second, she nodded. "Thank you. I'll take every prayer I can get right now."

They knelt next to each other on the padded cushion in front of the Martyrdom site of Thomas Becket. Morgan could feel the Dean's warmth by her side, and although his head was bowed, she sensed his silent prayer. She could only hope that his intercession might stop whatever curse the Black Anchorite had called down upon her.

Jake believed the words to be worthless, but Morgan still felt an icy hand around her heart, a chilling promise that she couldn't stop from filling her nightmares.

But when the darkness came, she would be ready, and she knew Jake would be by her side.

THE END

ENJOYED TOMB OF RELICS?

Thanks for joining Morgan, Jake and the ARKANE team. The adventures continue ...

If you loved the book and have a moment to spare, I would really appreciate a short review on the page where you bought the book.

Your help in spreading the word is gratefully appreciated and reviews make a huge difference to helping new readers find the series. Thank you!

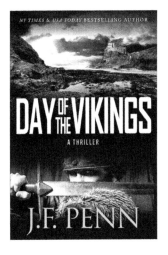

Get a free copy of the bestselling thriller, *Day of the Vikings*, ARKANE book 5, when you sign up to join my Reader's Group. You'll also be notified of new releases, giveaways and receive personal updates from behind the scenes of my thrillers.

WWW.JFPENN.COM/FREE

Day of the Vikings, an ARKANE thriller

A ritual murder on a remote island under the shifting skies of the aurora borealis.

A staff of power that can summon Ragnarok, the Viking apocalypse.

When Neo-Viking terrorists invade the British Museum in London to reclaim the staff of Skara Brae, ARKANE agent Dr. Morgan Sierra is trapped in the building along with hostages under mortal threat.

As the slaughter begins, Morgan works alongside psychic Blake Daniel to discern the past of the staff, dating back to islands invaded by the Vikings generations ago.

Can Morgan and Blake uncover the truth before Ragnarok is unleashed, consuming all in its wake?

Day of the Vikings is a fast-paced, supernatural thriller set in London and the islands of Orkney, Lindisfarne and Iona. Set in the present day, it resonates with the history and myth of the Vikings.

If you love an action-packed thriller,
you can get Day of the Vikings for free now:

WWW.JFPENN.COM/FREE

Day of the Vikings features Dr. Morgan Sierra from the ARKANE thrillers, and Blake Daniel from the London Crime Thrillers, but it is also a stand-alone novella that can be read and enjoyed separately.

AUTHOR'S NOTE

My story ideas always start with a place that resonates at some level and my international travels have driven the ARKANE series so far. The pandemic changed so much in our lives, including the ability to travel, so I had to set aside my book research plans and find an idea closer to home for this one.

Morgan and Jake will be back in another adventure and next time, I am determined to travel further afield for my book research!

You can see some of the pictures behind the book at www.pinterest.co.uk/jfpenn/tomb-of-relics/

Canterbury and the martyrdom of Thomas Becket

In October 2020, I walked the Pilgrims' Way from London to Canterbury following the route Becket took when he became archbishop and the paths that pilgrims traveled to his shrine after the martyrdom.

It was during a break in the pandemic lockdowns, and I was desperate to get out of the house. Walking outside for six days seemed like a good option and I hoped to find the thread of a story on the trip.

When I visited Canterbury Cathedral and attended sung Evensong, I decided to use the story of Thomas Becket, but not in the way that others have done. The historical details of

Becket's martyrdom are correct, but of course, the exploits of the knights after their banishment are fictional.

You can follow my path along the Pilgrims' Way at www.booksandtravel.page/pilgrims-way/ and listen to a solo podcast episode (or read the transcript) about the pilgrimage at:
www.booksandtravel.page/pilgrimage-canterbury/

Religious relics

Regular readers of my ARKANE novels will know of my obsession with religious relics. They continue to fascinate me and feature in many of my stories.

I went to the (delayed) exhibition about Thomas Becket at the British Museum in June 2021 and the final display case held the reliquary described in the book. I wondered whether it was really a piece of Becket's skull inside and if it wasn't, then whose could it be — and was it really medieval?

I also read the following books as part of my research:

- *Holy Bones, Holy Dust: How Relics Shaped the History of Medieval Europe* — Charles Freeman

- *The Relics of Thomas Becket: A True-Life Mystery* — John Butler

Processing of dead bodies

Human corpses provide an important service to the living and although there are strict laws around payment for body parts, the processing still needs to be done. I wrote Kelley's disassembly scene based on the following books:

- *Insider Trading: How Mortuaries, Medicine and Money*

Have Built a Global Market in Human Cadaver Parts — Naomi Pfeffer

- *Technologies of the Human Corpse* — John Troyer

- *The Red Market: On the Trail of the World's Organ Brokers, Bone Thieves, Blood Farmers, and Child Traffickers* — Scott Carney

To be clear, I am a registered donor and I want my physical body to be used after my death — ideally to help other people or advance medical science, but I wouldn't object to being turned into a relic!

Other aspects

I have not been to Cologne Cathedral or St Mary's Basilica in Kraków, but I spent many hours on various websites and virtual tours in an attempt to make my descriptions as exact as possible. They are both on my list to visit, as they are extraordinary places.

The quote on the tapestry in the citadel, "God will know his own," is attributed to the massacre at Béziers, France, in July 1209, when thousands of inhabitants were slaughtered indiscriminately as part of the Albigensian Crusade. I felt the phrase captured the spirit of the Crusades in general when so many were killed under the banner of faith regardless of their allegiance.

Why didn't I mention the COVID-19 pandemic?

Although I've set the story in present time, I decided to ignore masks, social distancing, vaccination, or any mention of the pandemic. My fiction is an escape from real life and hopefully, the complications of these few years will fade with time.

Use of AI and other tools

In an age where more and more text is generated with AI tools and creatives are increasingly AI-assisted, I think it's important to state usage in my books. I'm a techno-optimist and believe that AI tools can help authors become even more creative.

For *Tomb of Relics*, I used Google Search in addition to books for research; Sudowrite as an extended thesaurus to add to sensory description, although not for copying and pasting chunks of text; and ProWritingAid as part of my editing process. I also use Amazon for publishing, and Amazon auto-ads as well as Facebook for marketing.

If you're interested in AI and creativity, I have articles, interviews and resources at:
www.TheCreativePenn.com/future

MORE BOOKS BY J.F.PENN

Thanks for joining Morgan, Jake and the
ARKANE team. The adventures continue …

Stone of Fire #1
Crypt of Bone #2
Ark of Blood #3
One Day in Budapest #4
Day of the Vikings #5
Gates of Hell #6
One Day in New York #7
Destroyer of Worlds #8
End of Days #9
Valley of Dry Bones #10
Tree of Life #11
Tomb of Relics #12

Brooke and Daniel Psychological/Crime Thrillers

Desecration #1
Delirium #2
Deviance #3

Mapwalker Dark Fantasy Adventures

Map of Shadows #1
Map of Plagues #2
Map of the Impossible #3

Short Stories

A Thousand Fiendish Angels
The Dark Queen
Blood, Sweat, and Flame

Other Books

Risen Gods — co-written with J. Thorn

American Demon Hunters: Sacrifice — co-written with J. Thorn, Lindsay Buroker, and Zach Bohannon

More books coming soon ...

You can sign up to be notified of new releases, giveaways and pre-release specials - plus, get a free ebook!

www.JFPenn.com/free

If you loved the book and have a moment
to spare, I would really appreciate a short review
on the page where you bought the book.

Your help in spreading the word is gratefully
appreciated and reviews make a huge difference
to helping new readers find the series.

Thank you!

ABOUT J.F. PENN

J.F. Penn is the Award-nominated, New York Times and USA Today bestselling author of the ARKANE action adventure thrillers, Brooke & Daniel Psychological Thrillers, and the Mapwalker fantasy adventure series, as well as other stand-alone stories.

Her books weave together ancient artifacts, relics of power, international locations and adventure with an edge of the supernatural. Joanna lives in Bath, England and enjoys a nice G&T.

You can follow Joanna's book research and travels on Instagram and Facebook @jfpennauthor and also on her podcast at BooksAndTravel.page or on your favorite podcast app.

*   *   *

Sign up for your free thriller, *Day of the Vikings*, and updates from behind the scenes, research, and giveaways at:

www.JFPenn.com/free

*   *   *

Connect with Joanna:
www.JFPenn.com
joanna@JFPenn.com
www.Facebook.com/JFPennAuthor
www.Instagram.com/JFPennAuthor
www.BooksAndTravel.page

*   *   *

For writers:

Joanna's site, www.TheCreativePenn.com empowers authors with the knowledge they need to choose their creative future. Books and courses by Joanna Penn, as well as the award-winning *Creative Penn Podcast* provide information and inspiration on how to write, publish and market books, and make a living as a writer.

ACKNOWLEDGMENTS

Thanks to my patient readers who had to wait for this latest instalment of the ARKANE adventures. The pandemic threw a spanner in the works for all of us!

Thanks to Luke Purser for reading from the perspective of a medieval historian. Much love, always.

Thanks to Wendy Janes for edits, and Jane Dixon Smith for cover design and print formatting.

Printed in Great Britain
by Amazon

82567023R00079